GOTH GIRL

GOTH GIRL

MELANIE MOSHER

NIMBUS
PUBLISHING
nimbus.ca

Copyright © 2017, Melanie Mosher

All rights reserved. No part of this book may be reproduced, stored in a retrieval system or transmitted in any form or by any means without the prior written permission from the publisher, or, in the case of photocopying or other reprographic copying, permission from Access Copyright, 1 Yonge Street, Suite 1900, Toronto, Ontario M5E 1E5.

Nimbus Publishing Limited
3731 Mackintosh St, Halifax, NS, B3K 5A5
(902) 455-4286 nimbus.ca

Printed and bound in Canada

NB1268

Cover illustration: James Bentley
Design: Heather Bryan

Library and Archives Canada Cataloguing in Publication

Mosher, Melanie, author
Goth girl / Melanie Mosher.

Issued in print and electronic formats.
ISBN 978-1-77108-468-0 (softcover).— ISBN 978-1-77108-477-2 (HTML)

I. Title.

PS8626.O8426G68 2017   jC813'.6   C2016-908039-0
    C2016-908040-4

Nimbus Publishing acknowledges the financial support for its publishing activities from the Government of Canada, the Canada Council for the Arts, and from the Province of Nova Scotia. We are pleased to work in partnership with the Province of Nova Scotia to develop and promote our creative industries for the benefit of all Nova Scotians.

*To Jill and Sam,
two of my greatest teachers*

ONE

The salty smell of Halifax Harbour mixed with the aerosol stench of the paint, making my nose twitch. The night air was cool, even though summer was almost here. I was just minutes from home, in my favourite spot under the overpass. The vibrations of the traffic above and the adrenaline of being creative made me feel alive.

The surrounding noises faded away as I focused on the piece. The solid black outline I added made the colours pop. I had captured the feeling in my gut and displayed it for all to see. I nodded in approval, oblivious to the quiet crunching of tires on gravel. A sudden flashing of blue, red, and white light startled me and a siren broke my concentration. I dropped my cannon of spray paint, and listened as it rolled across the asphalt.

"Shit," I muttered to myself.

I took a deep breath, trying to slow my racing heart. *Act as tough as you look, Goth Girl.*

"Turn around, with your hands in the air," came a man's voice somewhere behind the light.

I tried to stand still, like I was unmoved by his command, but my knees shook.

"Turn around," the voice demanded. He was closer this time.
"Move the light so I can see," I shot back.
The light lowered slightly.
I turned slowly, placed my hands on my hips, and shifted my weight to my left foot. I snapped my gum loudly, thinking fast. I spotted my paint under the shoe of the cop shouting orders. A second cop sat in the car, watching everything.
"Put your hands up."
I didn't move. I hoped he wouldn't notice the beads of sweat forming on my forehead.
"Put your hands up, now," he growled again.
The light was too bright for me to see his face clearly, but I could see that his gun was still in the holster. His right hand was just a few inches above it, ready to move if needed. Staring at the piece, I swallowed, my tongue sticking to the roof of my mouth. Reluctantly, I raised my arms and spread my fingers.
"Are you responsible for this graffiti?"
I didn't even bother answering such a lame question.
"What's your name?" he asked, kicking my paint out of the way and stepping forward.
His breath reeked of stale coffee. I wondered if he had ever heard of a mint. "Picasso," I snapped.
"Don't be a smartass. You're coming to the station." He motioned toward the squad car.
Shit. I didn't know what else to do, so I smacked my gum, hoping it would drive the guy nuts like it did my science teacher. If I was going to the station, I wasn't going to make the trip a pleasant one.
He grabbed my arm and twisted it behind my back, forcing me to turn around. He took my other arm and pulled it down to meet the first. The cuffs clicked into place.
I looked at the graffiti I'd been working on. I wanted to remember every detail because I knew within weeks it would

be patched. The City of Halifax was quick about getting rid of unwanted art.

"Mind if I get a picture of this?" I nodded toward the wall I had just painted, thinking of my phone in my back pocket. The cop scoffed. "Yeah. Right." With one hand still on my arm and the other on top of my head, he placed me in the back of the cruiser and slammed the door.

A mix of smells bombarded me: alcohol, vomit, sweat, and stale cigarette smoke. There was a hint of cheap aftershave mixed in. I wondered if it belonged to the cop or one of his latest pick-ups.

I slumped in the seat. *I can't believe this.* I took a deep breath and let it out slowly. *How'd I get caught?* But I knew. I'd let the artwork get to me again. Every time I painted and tagged I felt content and free. The colours sprayed out of the cans and onto the concrete like magic. I could blend them together with ease, but I wasn't actually the artist: the art was travelling through me from another source. After all, that talent couldn't be mine. The shading I had managed brought the picture to life; I had created emotion on a concrete wall. And now I was on my way to the police station. I felt sick.

The cop got in, called in his arrest on the radio, and we headed downtown. My petty crime didn't warrant lights or sirens. I closed my eyes and thought of the first time I'd snuck out at night to do graffiti. I wasn't even out of the house for fifteen minutes. My heart pounded in my ears and I could barely hold the spray paint. When I shook the can, the rattle was so loud I stopped, certain everyone within a two-block radius could hear. I turned around and went home. That was a year ago.

The fluorescent lights of the station made me squint after the darkness of the night and the squad car. There were only a few other cops around. One of them nodded as we walked by.

The officer led me to a small wooden desk, plunked me down

on a hard chair in front of it, and then took a seat on the softer chair behind. He bumped the desk as he sat and a pen rolled to the edge and fell to the floor. I stooped to pick it up, forgetting my cuffs. I lost my balance and quickly stuck my foot forward to steady myself. I tried to move to a more comfortable position, but it was pointless with my hands trapped behind my back.

Seeing me squirming, the officer looked up. He got out of his chair and unlocked the cuffs. I wanted to rub my wrists, but I didn't want to let on that they had bothered me.

"What's your name?" he asked, booting up the computer on his desk.

I stared at his name tag: *B. Mitchell.* Trying not to be obvious, I checked out his face: the grey stubble, dark circles under his eyes, and a few too many wrinkles made him look old.

I watched as he looked me over, like every adult I met.

He looked at my spiked black hair.

No, it's not my natural colour, I thought, imagining I could read his mind.

He looked at my face, noticing the heavy eyeliner and mascara. When he spotted my nose ring and lip-piercing, his hand automatically rubbed his own nose and mouth.

He scanned my clothes: a plain black T-shirt covered by a black sweatshirt, plain except for the broken zipper and the hole in the sleeve, black leggings, and black army-style boots laced over grey hunting socks. I'm sure he didn't notice the little artist easel pendent hanging from my shoelace.

Finally, the officer's gaze returned to my eyes. I stared at him, unblinking, waiting for the usual look of sad disappointment. But his eyes were different: he was studying me, trying to figure me out.

I shook my head. *Look all you want. You see my get-up and draw your own conclusions. Which is exactly why I wear it.* Mom says it's to draw attention to myself. Wrong. I wear it because that's all grown-ups see and *I* can be invisible. The thought of my mother drew me back to the present. Mom. She was going to flip out.

"I *said*: what's your name?" Mitchell's fist smacked the desk close to me.

I gave him my best what-the-hell-was-that-for? look. "Take it easy, man. The name is Vic. Victoria Markham." I was proud that I'd made him lose his cool.

"Address?"

"2310 Leeds Street."

"How old are you?"

"Fifteen."

"Date of birth?"

"August 31, 1998," I said. "Exactly a year after Princess Diana's death. Mom's a royal family fanatic. She would have called me Diana, but she said the memory was too painful. So she named me after Queen Victoria instead. She said she cried for hours the day I was born. Not for me, though: for Diana."

Man, I was babbling. "Sorry, TMI," I added.

"What?" The cop glanced up from the keyboard.

I shook my head. "Too Much Information."

"Oh. Well, royal family or not, we have to call your mother. What's your number?" He picked up the phone.

My heart sank. I sighed quietly and braced myself for Mom's reaction.

TWO

I watched as he dialled. Even though it wasn't even ten o'clock yet, Mom would be asleep. She always went to bed early; that's when I hit the road. I'd been sneaking out two or three times a week. At first I didn't even paint. I'd just look at the concrete wall in front of me, imagine the artwork I wanted to create, and then scold myself. Who was I kidding? I didn't have the guts to break the law or defy Mom.

Then things changed, and I seemed to disappoint Mom without even trying. I did the dishes but all she saw was my unmade bed. I did the laundry but she screamed that I didn't sort the colours properly. Sneaking out got easier. The air outside seemed different. It was easier to breathe, it was lighter. Anything could set Mom off, and I was on guard around her. Alone, under the overpass, I felt at ease.

The cop's voice interrupted my thoughts and I listened to the one side of the conversation I could hear.

"Hello. Mrs. Markham? Yes, this is Officer Mitchell with the Halifax Regional Police, and I have your daughter here." A pause. "Yes, Victoria. I need you to come down to the station." Another pause. "No, she's not hurt…Yes, I understand it is late…She was picked up for doing some graffiti." He rubbed the back of his neck and closed his eyes for a moment as he listened. Now he looked like I did when I listened to Mom: beat. Defeated. Done. Why did she have to ask so many questions? Couldn't she just do what any other mother would do and rush down to the station?

"We can talk more when you get here," he assured her. "Okay, then. See you shortly." He hung up.

I watched him shake his head as he keyed more information into the computer.

"We don't need to wait for her." I leaned forward in my chair. "I'm a big girl now. Give me the lecture and let's move on."

He smiled wryly. "It's not that easy. You're a minor."

"Whatever," I huffed, slumping back in the hard chair. Somehow I was old enough to buy groceries and cook meals, but I wasn't old enough to get reprimanded without my mother being present. I shook my head again.

"You know," said Officer Mitchell, turning to me, "your art was good back there, and I've seen lots. I even tried it a couple of times when I was a kid. But it's against the law to paint wherever you feel like it."

"What do you care?" I turned away, rolling my eyes. I couldn't believe he thought my work was good. A flicker of pride fluttered in my chest.

He sighed. "Look, I am just trying to help you out here. Lose the attitude. I gave you a compliment." He stared at me, waiting.

I looked down. "Thanks," I grunted. "What does it matter, though? It'll be gone in a couple of days." I remembered the last piece I did: the clear lines and the intense colours really grabbed your attention. But then, less than a week later, it was plastered over with ugly grey paint.

"That's my point. If you'd put that artistic energy to better use, it'd be around for others to enjoy."

I looked back at his weary face. As if he really cared about my artwork. "Yeah, right."

"There's a program here in the city — the Community Art Project. It's for kids like you." I shot him a look and he hurriedly continued: "You know, budding artists that need some...direction." I softened. "Right now, they're working on a mural along the boardwalk."

"So?" I'd seen that mural with the tall ships. It was good. I hadn't realized it was being done by kids. "I don't need any *direction*. I like to do what inspires me, not some paint-by-number." I wanted to paint my own designs and work alone. I sure didn't want to hang out with a bunch of kids I didn't even know. I thought of my last report card: decent marks, but lots of comments like "not a team player," "lacks social skills," and "needs to put more effort into getting along with others."

"Just think about it." Officer Mitchell turned back to his monitor. "It counts as community service, and I am strongly recommending it." He clicked the mouse a few times. "I see here this is your first offence, and community service is the standard sentence."

First offence, huh? I smirked inwardly. I guess his computer didn't know about all the tags and pieces I'd put up over the last year. I shouldn't have tried a piece with so much detail tonight. It took too long. Now, I had my first offence. The words sunk in. Was I going to have a criminal record? Would this affect my university applications? I didn't like being thought of as a criminal, but I sure wasn't going to let this pig know that.

I heard a door bang open and turned toward the commotion. Amongst the muffled voices, a familiar one rang out clearly.

"Where's my daughter?" Mom shouted at the officer who had risen to help her.

She scanned the room and spotted me at Officer Mitchell's desk. Ignoring the first officer, she stomped over to me. The look of sleep still clung to her: her hair was flat on one side and a few blanket lines hadn't quite faded from her cheek. She wore a long coat and shoes, but I could see the pajama pants she had been wearing earlier peeking out underneath the hem.

"What have you done now?" She glared at me like I was pond sludge.

"Hi, Mom. Nice to see you." I put on my best fake smile. "Let me introduce you to this nice policeman who gave me a lift here tonight." I gestured politely to Officer Mitchell. Maybe a little humour would help her lighten up.

"Don't be sassy, young lady," said Mom. "Do you know how late it is? I have to get up early to go to work, and this is the thanks I get." Mom turned toward the policeman. "Julia Markham," she said, putting her hand out. "Is she under arrest? Officer...Mitchell, is it?"

He stood up and shook her hand. "I did make the arrest, but I have the option of forgoing the vandalism charge if she takes part in some community service." He glanced at me before explaining the Community Art Project. "She'd be removing graffiti in the city and learning to paint in a more appropriate location."

"Victoria will do whatever you ask." Mom placed her hand on my shoulder.

"Not interested." I tried to extract myself from her grip, but she clamped tighter, digging her nails into my shoulder.

"Of course she's interested." Mom's thumb jabbed my collarbone as she spoke. "You just tell me when and where. If she's going to sneak out at night and cause trouble, she can certainly do whatever it takes to make things right."

"Are you sure?" Officer Mitchell paused, looking in my direction, waiting for me to respond.

"Positive." Mom said through clenched teeth.

"Whatever," I added. Man, I hated it when she answered for

me. I was old enough to make my own decisions, even if they weren't all good ones.

"Okay then. I'll make some calls," said Mitchell. He reached into one of the drawers in his desk and pulled out a slightly crumpled business card. "Here's my card if you have any questions." He handed it to Mom, and then looked at me. "Vic, you're free to leave with your mother. I suggest you make a real effort to stay out of trouble." He held out his hand for me to shake.

"Sure thing." I stood and glared at him. Without another word, I spun on my heel and marched away, leaving him with his hand stuck out.

"Teenagers," said Mom, apologizing. She pocketed his card. "Thanks for your number." She followed me out.

When she met me at the door, Mom grabbed my upper arm with all of her strength and hauled me down the street. Once I spotted the car, I yanked myself loose and walked ahead. I figured the drive home would be our usual poor attempt at conversation — Mom would talk and I was supposed to listen.

Before the key was even in the ignition, she started. "What do you have to say for yourself, young lady?"

I shrugged. "Nothing."

I could argue with the cop or even a teacher, but when it came to Mom, my fight was gone. I felt defeated before I began, so I didn't even bother. James had argued with her all the time and what good did that do? Besides, Mom rarely listened to what I had to say.

She heaved one of her heavy sighs, started the car, and pulled away from the curb. "I can't believe you were traipsing around at night breaking the law. How could you do this to me? What if people at the hospital find out my daughter is a criminal?" Mom clung to the steering wheel with both hands and looked over at me.

"Yeah. Like I care what the people at your work think." I watched the lights whizzing by.

I caught a glimpse of graffiti and grinned. Some of it was sloppy. Lazy. It needed to be covered. But good street art — the grand scale and exaggerated images — I love the look of work like that. A while ago I'd watched a TV show called *Street SmART,* where a bunch of contestants competed each week doing different styles of graffiti that were judged by professional artists. One by one, contestants were eliminated, leaving the last one to win $100,000. They made it look simple, but good graffiti is hard to do. I found that out when I began to paint. You can't spray too heavy or the lines will drip; you have to be quick and decisive. And since you're working so close, you have to be able to see the finished product in your head as if you were standing back, admiring it. It's bigger than painting on a canvas. Much bigger. And better.

"There's nothing to smile about." Mom's face tightened as she clenched her teeth.

"The cop said my art was good." I closed my eyes, trying to get back the feeling I had when I was under the overpass — the cold can in my hand, the *swish* of the paint rushing out, a piece of art coming to life before me.

"Don't even talk to me about painting." Her knuckles turned white from gripping the steering wheel so hard. "You'll take part in that art program and then that's the end of painting." She sighed again. "I don't have the energy to argue with you, Victoria."

I began to protest, but she cut me off with a look. As if she could force me to change if she glared hard enough. *Nope, it's still just me, your disappointing daughter here. Still wearing the black clothes and the nose ring.* I went back to staring out the window and ignored her for the rest of the drive home.

Once we got home I went straight to my room and flopped on my bed on my stomach, exhausted. Truth is, I was really scared tonight. It hurt when Officer Mitchell grabbed my arm and twisted, but I had tried not to flinch or tear up. There was no way I was going to let him get the better of me. He was old and cranky. Tired of being a cop, I bet. And Mom — she was pissed. What else was new? But I never planned on getting caught. Now I had a record.

I flipped onto my back and stared at the stucco on the ceiling. It reminded me of paint on concrete. I tried to forget about the illegal part and just focus on the graffiti I had created. I got better and better each time. The persistence had paid off. And even though I spent hours and hours developing my skills, it never felt like work. The colours and lines in this latest picture were great. My backpack was stuffed with cannons and I had used them all: neon pink and green, bright blue and yellow, ruby red and burnt orange. My white highlights and black outlines were spot on. The idea was bold and imaginative; there wasn't anything else like it in the city. No other artist had the guts to include themselves in the piece. There, on a cold concrete surface, I had depicted my cold hard reality for all to see — at least for a few days. I thought about going back to get a picture. I should be building a portfolio of my work. Maybe Mom was determined about the community service, but I was determined about something too — I was definitely going to keep painting.

Three

In the morning, I made my way to the kitchen, dropped two slices of bread in the toaster, and pushed the lever down. I took a glass from the cupboard and poured some orange juice. I could smell a hint of the apple-cinnamon oatmeal Mom had made before leaving for the early shift at the IWK, the children's hospital. Our small kitchen was quiet except for the *tick-tock* of the old-fashioned wall clock and the hum of the fridge. No father. No mother. No brothers or sisters. Not even a dog or a cat.

There were some good things about being by myself: I didn't have to wash many dishes or pick up the dirty socks James used to always leave in the living room. I could even eat my breakfast in front of the television if I wanted. I didn't, because the picture above the couch gave me the creeps.

There was a day last year when I had come home from school to find Mom hanging that creepy print of Queen Elizabeth and Prince Philip — stiff smiles, jewels, furs, and all — in the living room. Mom's eyes were bloodshot and her hands trembled.

"What's going on?" I asked. "Where's the picture James painted?" He wouldn't like her moving his art.

Mom didn't respond.

There, in the middle of the floor, was a pile of busted paintings. Broken sunsets. Smashed frames. Everything James had painted in the last two years tossed in a haphazard heap. I stared at the broken pieces, thinking of James, the *artiste*. When he painted, he was so focused he forgot the rest of the world. That pissed Mom off.

"Mom…where's James?"

She looked at me helplessly. She didn't say the words out loud, but the look in her eyes told me he was gone. I knew they had loads of arguments about money and all the time he spent painting, but I never thought he'd leave Mom. Or me.

Mom had always liked the royal family, but when James left she went overboard.

"They're the only family we need, Victoria," she insisted.

Instead of landscapes and country scenes, I now have the Queen and her ancient husband in the living room and Prince Charles and Lady Diana in the hallway. It's creepy the way their eyes follow me as I walk by. If I stop they look down their noses in disgust. Yet, they are the ones standing in a forced pose with stiff smiles that don't quite reach their eyes.

James was the only father I ever knew, even though we didn't share any DNA. My real dad died shortly after I was born. James loved to paint and he began teaching me when I was five years old. At first we just used finger-paints….

"Like this," James said, trying to get me to mimic his picture — a little house, three stick people, a big tree in the yard, a golden sun.

I swirled the colours together on my paper: blue, green, red, yellow. I loved the slippery feel of the paint as it moved across the paper. Soon it was a big blob of greyish paint. I looked up at James.

"A true artist," he said, laughing. "You have your own ideas, and that's that."

James took a paint-covered finger and dabbed the end of my nose. I shrieked and giggled.

We continued to paint and chat for hours, swapping ideas and talking about what we were creating. When we finished, James carried me on his shoulders to the kitchen where we made messy ice cream sundaes, the chocolate syrup replacing the paint. The perfect way to celebrate our accomplishments.

I snapped out of my reverie. Years after the finger painting, James had introduced me to acrylics and oils. He showed me how to use the different brushes and knives.

When James left, he took his easels, tubes of paint, buckets of brushes, and pile of pre-stretched canvases with him. So I decided to buy my own. Only I decided to be more daring. Anyone could paint on a canvas, but not everyone had the guts to do graffiti. Over the past year I'd practiced and improved, learning to use the cans and different caps. I started with just my tag but kept at it, and soon I was creating full pictures and scenes — works of legitimate art. In the beginning it reminded me of James, but now it's more than that: I get pulled into the creative process and for a little while, it's all that matters....

But Mom associates painting with James and has vowed to remove all signs of both from our lives.

Breakfast done, I returned to my room to get dressed. I stood in front of the mirror and ran my gel-filled hands through my hair, pulling sections up to make them stand in familiar spikes. I smeared white foundation on my face, quickly lined my eyes with a black kohl liner, and expertly layered on the mascara. Like my spray-paint skills, my knack for going goth was getting better and faster. I slipped away and let Goth Girl emerge.

The first time Mom saw me with the goth look was a couple of months after James left. I needed a change, and I wanted something to focus on rather than the emptiness. I found a picture in a magazine and copied the look. But, wow, Mom freaked that I had gotten my lip and nose pierced. And she couldn't understand the makeup and hair.

"What have you done?" she hollered, her eyes wide with shock.

"I'm trying something new."

I had to admit I did get some satisfaction in making her lose her cool. Most of the time she acted like she didn't even know I existed unless she was yelling at me for something. At least now she could see me — or Goth Girl, anyway.

There was comfort in being Goth Girl: she was strong when I wasn't; she was mouthy when I was vulnerable; I missed James, she missed no one; I wanted Mom to understand me, Goth Girl didn't need anyone. I had considered giving up the look, but Mom was unreasonable.

"Take it off," she demanded. "Take it off now. You look like a no-good criminal." She studied me for a moment, narrowing her eyes. "You're not in trouble, are you? Are you taking drugs?"

"No! It's just a new look." I crossed my arms over my chest watching Mom freak. I stared at her, daring her to look away. Eventually she did.

"I don't understand you, Victoria." Then she sighed one of her "oh, poor me" sighs and left the room.

Never did she suggest I was too pretty to hide, or beautiful just the way I was. She still didn't see *me*. She never saw me anymore. When James was here Mom and I hung out and did "girly stuff" like painting our nails or doing each other's hair. But now it was always about her. Well, at least this way — when I had all the makeup on — her reaction was somewhat understandable. It was clear I was never going to please her, so I might as well please myself.

I stared at the only real family photo we had, tucked in the corner of my mirror. It was a strip of four shots of Mom and me from the photo booth at the mall. The edges were curled and the colours faded. I had begged Mom to get in the booth and she did, but she refused to smile. She and James had just had a big fight about something. She had taken me to the mall so she could get away from him for a bit, but it wasn't our usual shopping-and-splitting-a-milkshake-type day. I tried to cheer her up and I made a goofy face in each photo, sticking out my tongue and crossing my eyes. I tried to tickle her, but she got upset. The last picture is of me and a glimpse of Mom's arm as she escapes through the curtain, back to the mall.

And now Mom was angry with me over the graffiti. *I bet she wants to escape again and leave, just like James.* I opened my closet and reached for a black shirt and black jeans, leaving anything with colour pushed to the back, untouched.

FOUR

I grabbed my English books from my locker and headed down the hall, ignoring the people gawking at me. You'd think they'd be over it by now. After all, it's almost the end of the school year. I watched this couple approach, so into each other the building could have fallen down around them and they probably wouldn't have noticed. But when they got close, they stopped dead in their tracks and stared at me. I blew her a kiss and winked at him. When a girl coming up behind them didn't see them stop and crashed into them, I laughed out loud.

I like school. At least, I like the learning part. Some teachers say I have an "attitude problem," but they can't fault my grades. I get good marks; they're my ticket out of here. Maybe I'll head to a big city like New York and go to art school. I could stay there and get paid for creating art. It'd be great to live in a city that big with so much to see and do. I bet no one would even notice me there. I would just be another person walking down the sidewalk. I could paint in Central Park or on Staten Island and sell gallery prints of landscapes, like the ones James taught me to do. But my full-time job would be street art. I'd find a way to do graffiti and get paid for it — big billboard-type pieces used for branding and advertisement, full-sized walls commissioned by huge corporations and rich art enthusiasts. Even I was willing to be part of the "big-business-bullshit" world if it meant I could paint every day.

Yeah, right. Who was I kidding? New York was out of my league and way too expensive. I'd have to settle for the Nova Scotia College of Art and Design here in Halifax. But even that was over two years away. I had to get through the rest of high school first.

I slid into my seat just as the bell rang.

"Oh, look," said Mark, who sat in the next seat. "Today, for a change, Miss Vic is wearing *black*."

He snickered and Jeremy joined in.

"No, wait," said Kate. "Do I see a hint of colour?" She stretched her neck out like a goose to look at me. She flipped her hair and scoffed as she turned back around. "Never mind, it's just the light reflecting off her nose ring."

I didn't respond. It was the same thing every day and it had gotten old. Couldn't they come up with some new material?

Mr. Fawthrope walked in. "I have your papers graded," he said. "Some of you did very well. A couple of you need to see me after class."

He walked up and down the aisles, handing back papers. My eyes followed his every step. I tapped my pencil so hard I thought it might break. I'd stayed up late working on the assignment and even skipped going out to paint that night. I really liked Mr. Fawthrope; he wasn't like the other teachers. He encouraged us to think on our own and not just give the expected answer. He never followed the same boring script the other teachers used. The other teachers seemed to dislike him for this, but he continued anyway, and the school board allowed him to stay because his students did well.

"Great job," said Mr. Fawthrope, handing me my paper.

"Nothing to it," I said. I nodded and looked at the *A* circled in blue ink at the top of the page. I breathed a sigh of relief and tried to stuff the graded paper in my binder before Kate or Mark could see it. Usually I managed this without incident, but today I was not so lucky.

Mr. Fawthrope was still returning papers.

"How'd you get an *A*?" asked Mark, sceptical.

"What do you care?"

"There's *no* way you turned in a better paper than me," hissed Kate. Kate was the girl destined to be valedictorian. She was on every committee going, she played volleyball and basketball, she got top grades in every class, and she competed with anyone who tried to outdo her. I could not believe how important it was for her to be better than everyone else. I did a good job because I liked to learn; Kate's goal was to be the best. Even if it meant being the best snob.

"I worked hard." I gave Kate my best *screw you* look.

"Sure you did," she whispered back, rolling her eyes. "When do you have time? You're too busy painting graffiti at night." She glanced at Mr. Fawthrope and continued: "My brother said he saw you at the overpass the other day. And it wasn't the first time either."

"Tell your brother, thanks for the concern but I can look after myself," I snapped. *Shut up and mind your own business*, I thought furiously. I looked around to see if anyone else was listening.

"Jeeze. Fine. Relax. What about the paper?" asked Kate.

Man, she was persistent. "You can get papers online, Kate. They even sell papers better than yours. If fact, that's how you order them: less-than-Kate, as-good-as-Kate, or better-than-Kate. I was feeling spunky, so I ordered the 'better-than' option this time."

Kate flushed and opened her mouth to retort, but Mr. Fawthrope was already back at the front of the class talking about our next assignment.

At lunchtime, I sat in the cafeteria with Justine. Justine wasn't really a friend, just someone to sit with during lunch. We were in a couple of the same classes and even worked on a history project together last fall when she had just moved here. Most kids didn't seem to take to her fuchsia mohawk, dog tags, and heavy metal T-shirts. When it came time to pick a partner for the project, she picked me. It was the first time I got chosen because of the way I looked and the good feeling stuck with me. We got a great mark and started sitting together at lunch.

We weren't part of a clique — the jocks, the brainiacs, the socialites — but being excluded was one of the few things we did have in common. We had discussed the basics: I was an only child; she had two brothers. My dad had died and James had left; she lived with her mom and dad. She was into music; I was into art.

Justine took out one of her ear buds and handed it to me. "Here. Listen. I found a song by Motörhead that I hadn't heard before. It's awesome."

I put in the ear bud as she jacked up the volume on her iPhone. I grimaced and shook my head, handing her back the ear piece. We definitely didn't share a taste in music. "Aren't those guys old?"

"Music doesn't age." Justine moved back and forth with the beat, leaving one ear bud in place so she could continue to listen to the song as we sat.

I smiled. "So what's up, besides the new tunes?" I began stuffing fries into my mouth.

"Not much. I hear you're putting the paint to good use. Sorry you got nabbed."

I shrugged one shoulder. "Yeah. News travels fast around here."

"Jeremy's dad has a police scanner and hears everything. And Jeremy can't wait to tell."

I nodded in agreement. That was Jeremy. "Getting caught was just my dumb luck. You should've seen the piece, though. It was coming along great. Now I've got to paint some mural with a bunch of brats for community service." I took a gulp of Coke. "You know those mural paintings downtown? They're done by other 'bad' kids like me. It's called The Community Art Project or something lame like that."

"Cool. At least you will get to paint. Maybe you'll make friends."

I laughed hollowly. "With all the friends I have here, who has time for more? You know Kate and I are just like this," I said, crossing my fingers.

Justine chuckled and picked up her tray, pocketing her iPhone. "I'll see you later," she said. "And be careful. If you land in the slammer, who will I eat lunch with?"

After school I had to go to work at the convenience store down the road from my house. I look after customers, show them where to find things when they ask, ring in their purchases, and make change. When it isn't busy I sweep the floor and stock shelves. It's not exactly meaningful work but I'm grateful to have a job. I had gone to several interviews, but most bosses are small-minded and couldn't get past my wardrobe and makeup. One even had the nerve to predict I would never get hired "looking like that." Even Mr. Habib thought I looked like a hoodlum, but he's known me since I was little and said he knew I was a good kid. He figured if he hired me it would keep the real hoodlums from bothering his store. Whatever. I'm glad to have the money — paint and caps are expensive.

Mr. Habib was stocking shelves with toilet tissue and paper towels when I walked in. He was almost buried by cardboard boxes when he saw me.

"Hello, Victoria." He was the only one in the store.

"Hey," I said and went out back to grab an apron. I tied it around my waist. I didn't do anything that required an apron, but Mr. Habib considered it a uniform, and insisted I wear it.

"Then people know you work here," he'd say.

I was counting the cash in my till when I heard the door chime and looked up.

"Hello, dear." It was one of our regulars. A charming little woman all dressed in her best old-lady-polyester stretch pants, her grey curls freshly set. She was always very pleasant to me despite my appearance. It wasn't something I was used to.

"How many chocolate bars today?" I smiled. This lady came in at least twice a week and always picked up two or three: Mars Bars and Coffee Crisps. Always the same kind. I wondered who had the sweet tooth. Was it her? I would have asked, but Mr. Habib said it was none of our business what the patrons bought, as long as they paid.

"Oh, I think I'll just get two today," she said, selecting a couple of Mars Bars. "They're my son's favourite."

Question answered. I nodded.

"How was school today?"

"I got an *A* on a paper I worked really hard on," I told her. "That was good." It was nice to have somebody ask who seemed to genuinely care.

"That's wonderful." She smiled her dear-old-granny smile.

I couldn't help but smile back. "You know," I said quietly, "you can get these at Costco for a lot cheaper."

"I know. I tried that, but my son found the box and ate the whole thing in a couple of days."

"I'd do the same thing. Mars Bars are my favourite, too."

She laughed, took her change, gathered up the plastic bag, and headed out the door. "See you soon," she called with a wave.

"Sure thing."

Next into the store were three boys, younger than me, who I didn't recognize. They walked up and down the aisles but never made any motion to buy anything. They kept looking back at me and whispering. I was just about to tell them if they weren't going to buy anything to clear the hell out when Mr. Habib came around the corner. I swallowed the insult.

"Can I help you, boys?" Mr. Habib looked each one in the eye. He didn't like kids hanging around or who didn't buy anything.

One guy picked a pop out of the cooler and raised it up toward Mr. Habib like he was going to give a toast. "Just gettin' a drink."

Mr. Habib frowned and stood there for a minute, watching, before returning to the back room.

At the counter, the guys were fidgeting as they got their money out.

"What's up?" I asked.

"We heard you might be able to score us some cannons."

I narrowed my eyes. "Yeah. And what are you hoping to do with the paint?" These guys didn't strike me as budding artists. I scanned the bottle of pop. "That's a dollar seventy-five."

The boys were clearly relieved that I knew what they were talking about. "We want to teach ol' man Phillips a lesson," said the first boy, digging in his pocket for a toonie.

"He's our principal," added the second.

"Yeah," piped up the third boy. "He gave us detention for a week just because we banged up a couple of lockers."

The first boy leaned over the counter, dropped the toonie in my hand, and whispered. "We're gonna tag his house."

And this is what gives graffiti a bad name, I thought. I gave the first guy his quarter in change.

"Sorry, guys. There's a city bylaw that says no spray paint to minors. And there's no loitering in the store." I nodded to the exit.

"Thanks for nothin' weirdo." They slammed the door behind them.

Five

On Saturday morning, I walked to the address Officer Mitchell had given me. I enjoy walking. I hate the bus with all those people jammed into a small space like sardines...sometimes it doesn't smell much better than canned fish either.

I passed Mr. Habib's store. He was in the doorway, shaking a mat with one hand and holding the broom in the other. He tried to put the mat back in place but it got caught in the half-opened door. I grabbed the door handle and pulled, releasing the mat so he could continue to sweep. He nodded in thanks. I waved and walked on.

I stopped at Tim's and grabbed a coffee: double double, just like James. I hated the taste of coffee when he used to offer me one — bitter and strong — but now I liked the warm feeling it gave me. Plus the caffeine helps me stay awake after a night of tagging. Two old dolls waiting in line gave me a once-over, shook their heads, and clicked their tongues: "tsk, tsk." I just nodded at them and I continued on my way.

It took about twenty minutes to get to the address Mitchell had written down. I looked up at the office building and then checked the piece of paper — twice. There wasn't anything to be painted here, and there was no graffiti to be removed. I thought we were supposed to be painting outside. That cop probably fed me a bunch of bull. Figures. I rolled my eyes and stormed into the building, making the glass in the door rattle.

I marched over to the board listing the companies and the floors they were on, ignoring the lady sitting at the information desk in the lobby. She raised her head and looked me up and down over the glasses that balanced on the end of her nose. "Youth group? Third floor," she chirped.

"Excuse me?" I asked, even though I heard her clearly. I jabbed the up arrow for the elevator.

"I assume you are looking for the youth art program?" Her squeaky voice, like nails on a chalkboard, made the hair on the back of my neck stand up. "It's on the third floor."

"Oh no," I snarled. "I'm here for a job interview. I'm meeting the building manager on the sixth floor. He's looking for a fresh, non-judgemental person for the information desk." I entered the elevator and watched the lady huff and adjust her glasses. I blew her a kiss as the doors shut.

When the elevator doors opened on the third floor, I could see a few kids over to the right, standing around awkwardly. These must be my literal partners in crime. I moved to the left and leaned against the wall, out of the way. I thought of all the places I'd rather be: home in my room, school, work, or under the overpass with my backpack full of cans and caps. I smiled at the irony. That's what got me here in the first place.

The office door across from me opened to reveal a short woman who looked like the "before" picture on one of those makeover shows. Her clothes, a sweatshirt and jeans, were boring, run-of-the-mill, Value Village sale items. She wore no makeup and her hair had no real style. Plain. I wondered if her name was Jane.

"This way guys," she gestured to the office behind her. "Come on in. I'm Cathy and I am the facilitator for the Community Art Project."

I listened to feet scuff across the carpet, stalling, not wanting to move forward. Like cattle to the slaughter. Reluctantly, I followed.

"Have a seat." Cathy motioned to the office chairs surrounding a large table. In front of each place was a piece of paper and a couple of pencils. Two guys and two girls, including me, sat.

"I'll stand," said the third guy. He stood, back to the wall, with his arms folded over his chest. He didn't look any more interested in being here than I did. He also looked about my age, but that's where the similarities ended. He oozed money. Every bit of his clothing was brand-name. His hair was perfect. He stood with his thumbs in the pockets of his expensive jeans, while his jacket hung open to reveal a Polo Ralph Lauren shirt. He didn't even bother to take off his Oakley sunglasses. Spoiled rich kid.

"And your name?" asked Cathy.

"Zach." It was more of a grunt than a word.

"Nice to meet you, Zach." She then went around the room and asked each of us our names. I looked around the table as the others answered.

"Russell."

"Peter."

"Rachael."

"Vic," I said.

Everyone seemed to share the same lack of enthusiasm.

Rachael sparkled and shone like a porcelain doll, complete with eyelashes that fluttered as she spoke. I bet she thought her long, flowing, blonde hair hypnotized the boys and her tinkling laugh made them drool. *Give me a break.* I'd seen her type before and it made me nauseous.

Russell and Peter were two of a kind. When they were waiting outside the office, I noticed their pants hung low on their hips and bunched at their ankles. Did they think anyone wanted to see their underwear? Russell's shirt had a Green Lantern symbol and Peter's had an Angry Birds character. The biggest difference between them was their hair: Russell had curly brown locks that almost reached his shoulders and Peter's hair was reddish and cropped close to his head. They nodded at each other and did a fist bump; they must be buddies: Dumb and Dumber.

I shook my head and surveyed the room. The furniture was sparse: a tiny desk in the corner that must be Cathy's and the long table where we were sitting. Three of the walls were plain white, each with an ugly abstract painting; boring mixtures of browns, greens, and beiges. The earthy tones were dull and muted, giving me the urge to grab some spray paint and liven them up. The fourth wall was all windows. The sun shone brightly through the glass and I noticed the carpet in front of the window was faded. Natural light is great for painting, but too much reflection from the sun makes it hard to see your work. I frowned. *We should be outside instead of in this stuffy room.*

Cathy squinted in the sun, trying to see us all. She moved toward the window and reached for the chain to close the blind. She struggled to reach, so I jumped up and grabbed the chain for her.

When I turned back toward the group, Russell had his hand over his mouth and pretended to cough.

"Teacher's pet," said Peter at the same time as the coughing.

I shot him a look and bared my teeth as though they were fangs. "I don't like the sun," I quipped. "Or garlic."

"Or wooden stakes through the heart." Peter nodded, getting my drift.

I sat back in my chair, silently scolding myself. I shouldn't have been so quick to help.

"Now that you know each other's names, let's get started,"

said Cathy, sitting down and ignoring the banter between Peter and me.

"Aren't we supposed to be outside?" asked Zach, finally sliding his glasses up to rest on his head. He took off his jacket and flung it in the empty chair in front of him. I couldn't help but notice how the sleeves of his polo were tight around his biceps and his chest looked rock hard.

So, I wasn't the only one that wanted to get out of this room.

"We'll get to that. Today is about planning. We will be working on a semi-permanent painting for the fencing, or hoarding, that surrounds a construction site on Windsor Street." She gestured vaguely to the windows. "It's a few blocks from here. They're building new condominiums, so we're going to design a mural that represents what it means to live in Nova Scotia. It can be specific to Halifax or include the entire province. It can be about the past, the present, or the future. You'll have to decide, and you have to work together to come up with one mural, not a series of individual ones."

"How about we just paint a picture of ourselves being forced to paint against our will?" Zach smirked. Then he pretended to paint with one hand and tighten a noose with the other.

There was something about this guy I liked, despite his appearance.

"Well, Zach, I was hoping for an idea that would represent more than just the few of you in this room. We want it to speak to a larger population." Cathy looked around the table. "Any other ideas?" Her voice was calm and never changed, despite the attitude she got from Zach. I liked his approach, but I was also intrigued by her ability to ignore it. Maybe I would just sit back and listen as the day unfolded.

I wondered how Zach ended up here. And who showed up to paint dressed like that? But I liked that he had spoken first. I eyed Barbie and the two knobs, who never even opened their mouths to offer suggestions. I didn't speak up because I couldn't care less — I had no interest in sharing my ideas with these jerks — but I bet those three simply didn't have any ideas at all. Just empty space.

Rachael looked back at me with disgust in her eyes and wrinkled her nose. She had the nerve to judge me. *Well guess what, princess, at least I've got a brain. I bet your head is filled with nothing but hot air.*

She didn't speak but continued to glare. Finally, she tossed her perfect hair over her shoulder and looked down at the paper in front of her. She took a pencil and twirled it around in her hand a few times. I got bored of watching the yellow swirl of the pencil and stared at the bland brown paintings instead.

"So why all the makeup?" asked Russell, looking at me.

"What's it to you?"

He shrugged. "Just don't get it. Clearly it takes time and effort to do all that." He moved his finger in a circular motion around his own face. "And Rachael obviously spends time and energy, too. But the results are so different."

"Yeah. One you want to look at…and one you don't," Peter added. He nodded at Rachael, who smiled and blushed. Then Peter turned back to me and shook his head.

Cathy cleared her throat. "Any other ideas about the mural?" she asked again, trying to work past the bickering.

I looked up at her and then back over at Peter. "I'm okay with you not looking at me," I whispered, loud enough for him to hear. I raised my shoulders and gave him an oversized lame smile. *What did he even know about me?*

I grabbed the pencil in front of me and began to doodle — a few flowers, a cat, a bunch of innocent cows being led to an unmarked building. I glanced over and noticed Zach had finally taken a seat at the far end of the table away from the rest of us. He had even picked up a pencil. I looked around the table at the others and saw they were all sketching, ignoring Cathy's attempt at discussion. It seemed that, despite our differences, we all had at least one thing in common: we couldn't turn down the invitation of a blank piece of paper.

"Take your time," said Cathy. She got up from the table and settled behind her desk at her laptop and began typing. She seemed relaxed and unfazed by our talk and aimless doodling. I guess she gets this stuff from all the delinquents she meets. "We are spending three hours together each Saturday for the next two months."

"No way," said Zach, a bit too loud. His head flew up from his paper and he gave her a furious look. "I've got better things to do."

"What about my job?" I turned toward Cathy. She stopped typing and looked at me.

"Sorry. You'll have to make other arrangements."

"Don't do the crime if you can't do the time." Peter practically sang the words. "Suits me fine. The more I'm here the less I have to be at home with the old man."

I wondered what he meant by that, but I sure wasn't going to ask. All I could think of was trying to explain to Mr. Habib that I couldn't work Saturday mornings for the next two months.

I heard a quiet sniffle beside me and turned to see Rachael wipe at her nose with the back of her hand. She must have felt me staring because she looked up at me. I could see the shine of tears in her eyes.

It sucked having to be here, but I sure wouldn't cry over it. Especially not in front of other people. I reached out and touched Rachael's arm. "Aww. Does this mean you won't get the salon time you're used to?"

"Allergies." Rachael huffed and looked back down at her paper. "Freak."

No one spoke for a bit. We just doodled. Again, I looked

around the table and covertly eyed each paper. Rachael was alternating between her pencil and index finger. She'd make a few lines with the pencil and then blend with her finger. She wasn't done, but it was easy to tell she was drawing the Halifax waterfront. Peter was working on a dinosaur with scales and teeth so detailed it looked like it could leap off the page. Russell had sketched a guy on a skateboard and great letters in a really cool font that read, "Zoom." Zach was drawing a guy in a noose. *Wow, these guys are good.*

Cathy finally interrupted the silence. She hit a button and a screen came down over one wall. She tapped a few more buttons and a picture of the Tall Ships boardwalk mural appeared.

"This is one of the projects a previous group did," Cathy explained. She stood and moved around the room toward the screen. She held a small remote control in her hand. She changed the images as she spoke. "Here is another."

It was a picture that covered the whole wall of a brick building that must be a daycare. At least that's what the painting suggested: it showed kids playing on swings, skipping rope, and blowing bubbles. You could see the fun they were having just by looking at their faces. *Huh. Faces are hard.*

As the pictures changed I began to get excited despite myself. The next one was exactly my style: exaggerated cartoon-like images painted in bright hues with clear outlines. I started to get the same vibe I did when I was under the overpass — like I wanted to paint and nothing else. I took a deep breath and released it. I looked around at the others. I didn't want them to know how much painting meant to me. But I wondered if they felt the same way.

Rachael wasn't even looking at the screen. She was looking at her phone and admiring her manicured nails. Russell and Peter were looking at the pictures but it was hard to tell what they were thinking. Every once in a while Russell brushed the curls from his eyes, and Peter would tap his foot, but those were the only signs of life they showed. Then I looked at Zach. He was sitting up straight and focused. When the screen changed to the next picture he nodded and smiled. He really looked interested, even if he claimed not to be.

This was a chance to be a part of a really big piece of art that the whole city would see. I wanted to say, "Okay, I'm in." But I just sat there and said nothing.

"So what if we don't plan the mural?" asked Russell.

"Then it will be a long eight weeks." Cathy looked at each of us again. "You can all paint. We know that, because that's how you got here in the first place. Why not make a painting others can admire? The longer we spend here planning, the less time we have to actually produce the mural."

"Maybe we'll just slap some paint on the fence and call it a day." Peter looked like he had figured out a way to beat the system, and he was proud.

"Yeah, we'll say it's abstract art," added Russell. They both chuckled.

"I guess there's no stopping you from doing that," answered Cathy. "But keep in mind: your names will also be on the fence. Whether you do a good job or not is up to you." She hit the remote again and the screen went blank.

Russell stopped laughing and leaned over to Peter. "Cool. My name on a piece of art for all to see? I guess it wouldn't hurt to make it look good."

"True," said Peter. No one else spoke, but all five of us nodded.

Cathy made one last comment: "We are wrapping up early today because it's our first session, but I want you all to get a sketchpad and think of ideas over the next week. It will help make our next meeting more productive."

"Homework? Are you kidding?" Zach got up, took out his phone, and immediately headed for the door. He had his head down and was in such a hurry to leave, he walked right into me. "Oh. Sorry."

I tried to speak, but instead I felt myself blush. *Jeeze, keep it together, Vic.* His chest was hard and muscular. His eyes were the same bluish-green as deep ocean water in cheesy tourist ads for Caribbean vacation packages. I stared, searching for words, making a total fool of myself. I finally found my tongue again. "No problem." I moved aside so he could pass. But he didn't.

"How'd you end up here?" He looked me up and down. I wasn't sure if I should be flattered or insulted.

"I heard this was the most exciting place to be on a Saturday morning, so I begged them to let me be a part of the group."

Zach chuckled. His eyes sparkled when he laughed. "Really? That's exactly what I did. I guess it must be true." He paused, and then said, "So, do you like to paint?"

"Yeah. I like the look of good graffiti. I like the bold colours and the heavy lines." *Man, I was blabbering like an idiot.*

"Really? The bold colours?" A cocky smirk formed on his lips. "The only thing close to a bold colour on you is those beautiful blue eyes." My cheeks burned but I refused to look away. "But you like colour?" He shook his head and smiled. "Okay. If you say so."

"I *do* say so," I snapped. I wasn't sure if I was angry at him for being a jerk or at myself for being so sappy. What was up with this guy? He was everything I usually avoided: the brand-name clothes, the perfect hair, the movie-star teeth. His strong shoulders and hard muscles indicated hours spent at the gym with other meatheads. And yet, I smiled. Those eyes. And the way he had looked at the graf on the screen — he'd been completely absorbed. There was more to this rich kid than the way he looked.

"I gotta go. My dad's waiting for me. See ya next time." He flashed another smile.

His grin actually made me feel woozy.

Dammit.

Six

When I got home Mom was in the living room sitting on the couch sipping tea from a cup with Princess Diana's face on it. I wanted to walk by and go straight up to my room without getting interrogated, but no such luck.

"So, how was it?" asked Mom.

"Fine." I could feel my stomach start to knot and my shoulders get heavy. I knew she was going to ask a ton of questions I didn't feel like answering.

"Were you painting the whole time?"

The way she said *painting* made the hair on the back of my neck stand up. I glared at her. "No."

"Why not?"

"We have to plan the mural first, and no one wanted to speak up and give ideas."

"That's silly. Why didn't you just say what you thought?"

Ugh. Just stop already, Mom. "It's not that easy. They already think I'm a freak and a kiss-up." I didn't want to suggest something they didn't like and have them think I was stupid too.

Mom sighed, put her teacup on the coffee table, and got up from the couch. "Since when do you care what others think?

You sure don't care what I think, or you'd clean that stuff off your face and stay out of trouble."

So here we were — at the familiar impasse — not hearing or understanding each other. For a moment, I thought of the others around the table today. What was it like with their parents? Did Rachael get along with her mother? Did Russell bond with his dad? I thought I bonded with James. But obviously, not enough.

I felt reckless all of a sudden. "Do you miss him?" I asked her.

Mom looked like a cornered animal. "Who?"

She knew exactly who I was talking about.

"James."

"I don't want to talk about him. Stop trying to change the subject." Mom grabbed her cup and walked away. I heard her in the kitchen, clanging dishes and banging cupboard doors.

Questions buzzed in my head all week, making it hard to concentrate on anything else. How did Zach end up in the group? Was he picked up by the cops too? Did he have a girlfriend? He might be all pastel polo shirts and expensive watches, but he also had a pretty quick wit and lots of creative talent. Or maybe that was just for show. After all, that's kind of what I did. No one really knew what I was thinking — ever — because I'd mastered the art of a snarky clap-back and a blank expression whenever anyone said something that annoyed me. I was a good actor. Maybe Zach was too.

I picked up my math notebook and printed Z-A-C-H on the cover with plain capitals, then in cursive writing. I added curly tails and fancy strokes. I tried big bubble letters and large block letters. Some I left clear, some I shaded to create dimension. I even added colour to some. Before I knew it, the entire front of my book was covered in Zach's name. I started to blush.

Thankfully, I was alone in my room, and no one could see what I'd done.

I'd never felt this way before. It was strange, but exciting, like the adrenalin rush I get from tagging. Maybe Zach was a new way to feel a thrill. I tried to not think of him, but that just made it worse. I tried doing math homework and found myself wondering what he was doing. I tried to read but kept picturing him in that tight shirt. I tried to think about what I might paint if I went out, but when I thought of mixing colours I was reminded of Zach's turquoise eyes and cocky smile.

Dammit.

At lunchtime on Monday, I sat in my usual spot in the cafeteria with Justine.

"Hey," she said, pulling one ear bud from her ear as I sat down.

"Hi." I took a swig of milk.

"How did the 'painting with potential prisoners' go on the weekend?" she asked.

I was surprised Justine remembered. And I was impressed with her sense of humour — she rarely made jokes.

"Okay," I said. I shrugged and picked up my slice of pizza.

Justine nodded and went back to eating her lunch.

As I chewed, I thought of telling Justine more about the group. It was one thing not to talk to Mom, but there was no reason not to talk with Justine. We weren't really friends, but there was no harm in chatting.

"The other kids are kind of a drag. There's Russell and Peter. They're like twin punks. They laugh at each other's jokes and fist bump." I glanced at Justine and she rolled her eyes. I nodded. "Yup. Then there is Rachael. She is a living Barbie doll with perfect hair and manicured nails. She flirts with Russell and Peter and they practically drool over her. It's hilarious." I paused, trying to sound casual. "Then there's Zach. He looks like a spoiled rich kid, but…." I waved my hand in front of my face, trying to brush away my words. I didn't mean to word it like that.

Justine sat up straight, took out the other ear bud, and then leaned in closer. "Tell me more." She nodded encouragement.

"Nothing."

"You started to tell me so you might as well finish." Justine smiled, and she seemed sincere. So I spilled my guts.

"He wears nothing but brand names. You know, Under Armor pants with his Ralph Lauren shirt. His sunglasses cost more than my whole wardrobe. He obviously goes to the gym because he's built. But he's cocky with a sharp tongue, and kind of rude."

"And you like him," said Justine. It wasn't a question.

"No I don't." I said way too quickly.

Justine arched an eyebrow and tilted her head to side as if to say, "Yeah. Right."

"Well, I don't know if I do or not," I admitted, squirming in my seat a little.

"I say you do, and I know why."

"What do you mean?"

"'A sharp tongue and kind of rude?' Doesn't that sound like someone you know?" Justine stared at me.

I pointed my finger at my chest. "You mean me? No way, I'm always so sweet and full of manners. Maybe it's that opposites attract?" I laughed.

It felt good to talk to Justine. But conversations about boys and boyfriends made me uneasy. I had a thing for this guy, Tony, last year, but it never went anywhere. He sat with me a few times in the cafeteria, but that was it. His friends gave him a hard time for hanging out with a "girl who looked like that" so he ditched me. After that, I just kept to myself and didn't even think about dating. Until now."

"Whatever. I don't think I'm girlfriend material." I looked over at Justine. I'd never seen her with a guy, either, now that I thought about it. Another thing we had in common.

"Don't look at me," she put her hands up. "I'm not one to give dating advice."

I thought of Mom and James. I sure didn't learn anything about relationships from them: they argued most of the time. The only time they seemed genuinely happy was on Sunday nights when they'd curl up on the couch, eat popcorn, and watch old movies together. They both loved *Gone With the Wind* and *Casablanca*.

"I guess I'm on my own, then." I smiled and rolled my eyes.

"Maybe the best place to start is to actually talk to him," Justine suggested. We both laughed and spent the rest of lunch chatting before the bell rang.

On our way to history, we passed by Mark and Jeremy in the hall.

"Oooh look!" called Mark. "I think we have a new couple at school." He wolf-whistled and pointed to Justine and me.

"A couple of losers, you mean," said Jeremy.

Mark and Jeremy laughed at their own lame joke.

"Russell and Peter?" Justine looked at me and pointed back at the two boys still laughing.

"Exactly." I nodded. "Why do they always come in pairs?"

Justine shook her head as we entered the classroom.

Mr. Jones started talking about the history of Pier 21 in Halifax and the thousands of immigrants who landed here from all over the world. He talked about ancestors and how interesting it could be to trace families over generations. He said we should consider our own family trees and see if we could find any connection to Pier 21.

Stuff like this always bummed me out: I knew Mom was an only child and her parents lived in England, but I had never met them. Dad's side of the family was a complete blank, and James left. Guess there wasn't much to think about in the story of Vic Markham.

Soon my thoughts drifted to Zach and the mural. I stopped listening to Mr. Jones, tore a piece of loose leaf from my binder, and picked up my pencil. I liked the feeling of holding a pencil, moving it across the page, hearing the faint scratch of lead on paper, and watching as the picture came to life. I thought I was doodling aimlessly but before my eyes, a picture of Zach suddenly took shape. Once I realized what I was drawing, I tried to remember every detail — the broad shoulders in that tight shirt, the way he stood with his thumbs in his pockets, the cocky grin...those eyes. I sighed. The thought of those eyes that made me wriggle in my seat.

I wondered what kind of art he did. For me, graffiti always came out in a hurry — a sort of explosion of emotion — but this art project was going to be different. I was supposed to be taking the time to think carefully about the finished piece and what others would think of it. Mr. Jones's voice kept interrupting my daydream. Maybe we could we include history in the design of project? Maybe a sketchbook was a good idea after all. I decided when I got paid I'd go get one.

After school I strolled home thinking through ideas for the mural. I was enjoying the chance to be creative. The sun was out but there was still a bit of coolness in the spring air. Lawns were beginning to turn green, and muddy leaves clung to the edge of the sidewalks. Mom was outside cleaning spent blossoms and dead weeds from the flower bed by our front doorstep. She hadn't worked in the garden since James left. Maybe this was a good sign. I practically skipped up the driveway.

"Hey." I dropped my backpack and went over to kneel beside Mom. "Remember the year we planted sunflower seeds here?" I thought of the bright yellow petals and black seeds on tall stalks gently waving in the breeze.

"Yes." Mom looked at me and smiled. "You came out and checked on them every day to see if they had sprouted. You could hardly wait for them to come up through the dirt. I had to keep reminding you that you couldn't uncover them to see how they were doing."

"I know." I laughed and leaned against Mom's shoulder. It felt good, like old times. "I think you even took a picture with me beside the flowers when they finally bloomed. They were as tall as me."

"That's right," said Mom, nodding. I was glad she remembered too. "So, how was school?" She bent forward, again, digging in the soil.

"It was okay." I paused. "Mr. Jones was talking about Pier 21 and family trees. Did any of my relatives come to Canada through there?"

Mom sat back with her legs still bent beneath her. "No. I flew on a plane from England when I was twenty-one."

"What about Dad's side of the family?"

Mom's eyes instantly went from being filled with happy nostalgia to anger. "Look. Your dad's dead and I don't know anything about his family. I thought we had this conversation years ago." Mom got up and brushed off her pants.

"Jeeze, I was just thinking about it because Mr. Jones brought up the subject. Sorry I asked." *Way to overreact, Mom.* I stood up too. I guess there wasn't going to be any mother-daughter gardening today. So much for happy memories.

"Well, just forget it," Mom said. "I'm your family, and that's all you need."

How warm and comforting.

Mom stooped to gather her bucket and trowel. She turned and went into the house, letting the door slam shut behind her.

I trudged back to the driveway to get my backpack.

seven

On Friday I stopped into the store and picked up my paycheque. I hadn't planned on telling Mr. Habib about my illegal activity, but I had to explain to him why I couldn't work Saturdays for the next little bit. He wasn't happy about it, but he fixed the schedule so I'd work two weekday evenings or a Sunday instead.

"But don't let your grades slip," he warned.

Who does he think he is, my father? Oh yeah, I forgot. I don't have one of those.

He even tried to get me to talk about why I would break the law. "You are so smart, Victoria. Too smart for that." He shook his head and waved his hands as he talked.

"I know, but —"

"You have things rough, but that's no excuse." He looked me fiercely in the eye.

"Yes, but —"

"Everyone has rough. Me, I came to this country with nothing. But I work hard. And I'm grateful to have the opportunity. You have a talent. Use it. But use it for good. Good like you." He placed his hand on my shoulder and nodded. He believed what he was saying.

I swallowed my snarky retort and thanked him for the money and the advice. I hurried out of the store and down the sidewalk. It was four o'clock and the traffic was starting to build with people anxious to start their weekends early. I crossed a busy intersection and some guy waiting for a red light hollered at me out his window. Adults are so quick to judge. I flipped him off. *Judge this.*

I felt a twinge of guilt when I remembered Mr. Habib's words, but I quickly squashed it and picked up the pace. I wanted to get my sketchbook and start drawing as soon as possible.

I was thinking of what I might draw, which made me think of what I'd already created. I wasn't far from my favourite graf spot, so I veered off course. I had meant to come back before this and get a photograph of the piece I'd gotten caught doing. I wondered if the city had a chance to patch it yet. I hoped I wasn't too late.

I crawled over the guardrail and down the bank. I could smell the harbour and the zooming rush-hour traffic overhead. I couldn't tell if it was the vibrations of all the vehicles or my anticipation that was making my hands shake. I held my breath and rounded the corner slowly. I spotted some unfamiliar tags — I guess I wasn't the only one who used this spot. My eyes moved along the concrete toward my graffiti. I caught a glimpse of grey. My heart sank. The breath I was holding came out as a heavy sigh but still I forced one foot in front of the other.

And then, there it was. My art had not been covered, but simply hidden from my view by the angle of the sun. There was my masterpiece of bursting colours. Staring at it stirred up feelings of anger and frustration, then doubt and gullibility. Finally, I felt the determination of the girl in the piece and grabbed my phone. It was good, despite my doubts. It was also a good thing I didn't have my cannons with me or I might have had the urge to take them out and finish the piece. Daylight or not. Above or below the law. I smiled to myself. It was easy to think this way when I didn't have the option. I snapped a few pictures and made my way back up to the street.

Seeing my artwork inspired me, so I rushed to the store. I always came to this Walmart to buy my paint. Justine was one of the cashiers, and she knew about the stupid Halifax bylaw that said minors couldn't buy spray paint, but ever since we aced that history project last fall, she agreed to ring me through.

I found a sketchpad and got some new pencils too. I strolled through the ladies'-wear section and eyed the beautiful dresses. I felt the soft fabrics and even held different ones up under my chin to see what they might look like. None of them matched my spiked hair and pale skin.

"What are you doing?"

The gruff voice startled me. I turned and looked into the judging eyes of a security guard.

"I need a dress for prom," I said sweetly. I held up the lacy blue dress in my hand. "Does this one bring out my eyes?"

The guy stared at me. Hard.

Wow. Did he really think it was *that* unbelievable that I could go to the prom? I went to put the dress back on the rack but changed my mind. Attitudes like his just made me so mad. I held it up under my chin again. "You got a phone?" I asked.

"Yeah. Why?"

"So you can take a picture and stop staring." I let go of the dress and watched it crumple on the floor in front of me. I turned on my heel and stalked off toward the checkout.

EIGHT

The alarm buzzed in my ears. *Where am I?* I blinked a couple of times and stretched my arms over my head. The alarm kept buzzing. Slowly, I realized I was at home and it was my phone. I searched for it on my nightstand and finally made it shut up. I slumped back on my pillow. *It's Saturday; I don't have to get up for school and work's not for another few hours.*

"Shit!" I said aloud. *It's Saturday; I* do *have to get up for my police-mandated community service.*

I threw back the covers and my sketchpad fell to the floor. When I got home last night I had opened my brand new, creamy white sketchbook and began collecting ideas for the Community Art Project and for other paintings I might do someday. There had been times when the pencil in my hand could barely keep up with the images flashing through my head. These sketches were becoming a way to express all of my ideas and not just a way to vent my anger. I began to actually consider art school and thought maybe this could begin my portfolio. I still wasn't sure how I'd ever pay for school, but it couldn't hurt to think about it. I must have fallen asleep. Now, I was bone tired and late.

I flew around my room, quickly grabbing clothes and throwing them on. I pulled at my hair, trying to adjust the already gel-filled spikes that had flattened over night. I slapped on my makeup and rushed from the room. I skipped breakfast and didn't have time to stop at Tim's. I hurried into the building and went straight to the elevator. The same lady was at the lobby desk, and I gave her a sheepish grin as I passed by. I rushed into the room.

I glanced at my phone to check the time. Somehow I had managed to get here just under the wire. I searched for Zach. When our eyes met he smiled and my empty stomach lurched. I quickly took a seat.

Again, there were paper and pencils. And again, we all doodled automatically. The only sounds were scratching pencils and tapping erasers. I started sketching without thinking and it took me a minute to realize I was drawing Zach. I quickly covered it with dark strokes and looked around to see if anyone had noticed.

"Good morning, everyone." Cathy closed the door behind her. "So, are we ready to start designing our mural?"

No one said a word.

Cathy wasn't discouraged by the apparent lack of interest. "I want you to think about something." She looked around the room, making eye contact with each of us. "It's small, incremental steps that will lead to a large, breathtaking piece of art. There is the discussion, the planning, the sketches, the choice of colours and textures, the lighting, and the perspective. This mural is both a collaboration and a statement of each individual taking part."

"Sounds like a bunch of crap," muttered Zach. He sat back in his chair, putting his pencil down. He folded his arms across his chest. I wondered if he really felt that way. I'd seen the way he looked at the paintings on the screen last week.

"It might *sound* like crap, but it works," Cathy insisted as she moved around the room. "The first small step was the sketchbook. Did anyone bring one?"

Nobody answered, but my stomach tightened. I had filled pages and pages of my sketchbook, but I was glad I hadn't brought it with me. I didn't want to be the keener.

"So no one drew anything to do with the project?" Cathy asked. "I'm surprised. Most artists can't resist a new idea, even if they want to." She peered around the table. "It continues to play on their mind until they have to put it to paper."

I glanced around and everyone remained quiet. Peter squirmed in his seat and looked like he might say something but then he looked down at his shoes. His face was peppered with freckles and he had a mark on his neck that I couldn't help but stare at. I wondered if it was a birthmark or a bruise. He jiggled his left foot for a few seconds, contemplating. Then he shifted again and reached into his back pocket and pulled out a piece of paper. He unfolded it, put it down on the table in front of him, and smoothed out the wrinkles. "You said it was about living in Nova Scotia," he said, "so I drew an idea of where each of us might live."

There were five images: a castle, a dungeon, a jail cell, a gymnasium, and a trailer. I stared at the pictures. His concept was pretty cookie-cutter, but the detail was amazing. I figured I was meant for the dungeon because of the bats and the vampire he'd included. Rachael would get the castle, and Zach the gym. But I couldn't decide on the other two. Did Peter think of himself as a criminal or trailer trash? Either way, it wasn't much of a choice. I scrutinised him, trying to decide.

"What?" asked Peter.

"I don't think we need five places. We're having so much fun, let's all live together in the jail cell." I flashed him one of my lame smiles.

"Nope. That's just for me, according to my dad. Just a matter of time." Peter folded the paper quickly and stuffed back in his pocket, his ears reddening.

My stomach tightened again. I knew what it felt like to have a parent disappointed in you, and it wasn't great. It also sucked that I got arrested doing something I actually really cared about.

"Speak for yourself," I said. "I got nabbed, but I'm definitely not a criminal."

"Sorry to tell you this, but yeah, you are," said Russell. "We all are and that's why we're here." Russell looked at me and put his hands in the air.

I stared back at him. His eyes were as brown as the curly hair that almost reached his shoulders. Today's T-shirt had a picture of Stewie from *Family Guy* on it. It was clean but worn. I even noticed a hole in the seam by the collar. If I saw him somewhere on the street I would never think he was a lawbreaker — I'd also never know he was a talented artist. I glanced at Peter, Zach, and Rachael. I always imagine artists as sophisticated and self-assured, walking tall, and proud of who they are. A bit eccentric maybe, but confident. That didn't sound like any of us. But none of looked like criminals, either.

Well, except me, according to Mom.

I changed my mind and decided to fess up about my sketchbook. After all, if I had to paint I might as well have a say in it. Ever since that history class on Monday I kept going back to the idea of families through time.

"Well, I did get a book, but I didn't bring it." I paused and looked down at the pencil in my hands. "I was thinking we could do a collage of the different type of houses through history." I looked up to see what they thought.

Blank stares all around.

Come on people. I'm trying here. "You know: wigwams, a habitation, log cabins, barracks...." No one said a word. I stared at Zach and raised my eyebrows, wishing he'd at least make a comment.

"That could work," said Zach, as if he read my mind. "Maybe we could include a house made from stone like the ones in the North End." The Hydrostone houses had been built after the Halifax Explosion. Zach smiled at me.

I felt my face flush and I looked down at the table. *Whoa, where did that reaction come from?* I ignored the feeling of jelly in my stomach and breathed a sigh of relief when the others seemed to loosen up.

"Well, I think we should include a ship, since we have the Navy here," said Rachael. She tossed her golden locks around her shoulder and smoothed the front of her silky shirt.

"Maybe a university," suggested Russell, brushing curls from his eyes. "You know, to represent student housing?"

Cathy nodded. "This is wonderful. Let's sit down and get to work. We'll sketch out the ideas before we actually go to the site." She motioned for us to get going, and handed us fresh paper. Everyone went to work except Zach.

"Aren't you going to help?" Rachael asked Zach. She got up and moved over to sit beside him. After tossing her head so her hair swung around her left shoulder, she smiled and winked. I felt a hot stab of jealousy. Another reaction I didn't expect.

"Looks like you guys need all the help you can get." Zach stood up and moved toward the window. "This project sucks." He seemed unnerved by Rachael's flirting. I inwardly sighed in relief.

"Then help us out, man." Russell looked up and pushed his curly hair out of his eyes. "It's not like any of us want to be here." He offered Zach a pencil. "Might as well make the best of it."

Zach refused the pencil, so Russell tossed it back on the table and shrugged.

"At least we get to paint in the daylight for a change," said Peter. He gave Russell a high-five. Zach stayed at the window.

I agreed with Peter. Painting at night had its drawbacks — colours appeared dulled and sort of blended together, and little details disappeared in the darkness. But I kept quiet, because I didn't want to take sides against Zach. I liked my concept and watching everyone sketch was turning out to be okay. They each had some talent...maybe I could even learn something. It didn't mean I had to make friends. Especially with Rachael. Her flirting was really bugging me. I didn't know if anything would happen between Zach and me, but I sure didn't want her to be the reason it didn't.

The saying "keep your friends close and your enemies closer" flashed through my mind. I didn't have friends, but I might have an enemy. I moved to the seat beside Rachael.

I studied the sketch she was working on. She had a realistic style and it was good. The frigate looked almost ready to set sail. You could practically see the water move around the hull, and see the tiny rivets in the metal sheeting. There was even a helicopter launch pad.

"How long have you been drawing?" I couldn't imagine having the talent to draw like that. Her pictures looked like photographs.

"Forever," she sighed. "But I really like doing landscapes. Two years ago, on my fourteenth birthday, I got this art kit for painting scenery — I was hooked."

"Your work's great," I said honestly. Even if she was an airhead, she was a talented one.

She gave me a small smile. "Thanks. It's about the only thing I can seem to do right." Rachael stopped talking and continued to draw.

I didn't ask what she meant. I wasn't here to make friends.

Russell and Peter were working side by side. Russell used tubes and arrows in his work and included a lot of lettering. Peter's style was all in the shading. I heard him telling Russell that he only ever used black and white. It was pretty cool what he could do without any colour. The two kept talking, but I stopped listening. Zach had sat back down, but he stayed on his own, doodling silently.

I kept looking at him, hoping to catch his eye. I cleared my throat. Nothing. I was interested in him, that I knew for sure. What I didn't know was if he would be interested in me. I thought of Tony and my heart sank. But then I reasoned that, with Zach's cocky attitude, he probably wouldn't care what others said. He might even date me just to spite his friends. I smiled at the thought. Finally, I faked a cough and he looked my way. He nodded. I felt my cheeks heat up and was grateful for my makeup. I quickly looked down and tried to focus on the sketching.

Before I knew it, Cathy was announcing it was time to pack up for the day.

"Hey," I said to Zach on my way out. I was hoping to talk to him but a single word was all I could manage.

"Hey." But just then, his phone rang. He glanced at the screen and then back at me. "I gotta go. Come a few minutes early next week and we can talk." He grimaced at the caller ID and left.

Yes. I floated from the room.

Nine

Monday was busy. I aced a science test and worked at the store after school. Then I stayed up late to finish a history assignment and passed it in on Tuesday. I was glad when school was over for the day and I hurried home. The house was empty. Usually Mom was home by now, but not today. I took the mail from the box and flipped quickly through the pile: bills, flyers...and one small white envelope the size of a card with handwriting I didn't recognize. I dropped the pile on the kitchen table and decided to get supper ready. Mom was a terrible cook. She used to leave the meals up to James. I tried to help out but Mom was hard to please, and I often just didn't have time.

Mom barged in just as I was closing the oven door. "What are you up to?"

"I'm making oven-fried chicken." I stood proud and grabbed the wet dishcloth from the sink and began wiping up the spilled flour and spices from the countertop.

"Oh. Sorry. I should have called. I'm going out with some of the girls from work." She fidgeted with a thread on her sleeve. "Thanks, anyway." My stomach dropped and I just stood there staring at her. She shrugged. "They're picking me up here, so, do you mind cleaning this up?" She motioned toward the mess on the counter.

I didn't speak, but the voice in my head was screaming. *What the hell?! I just cooked a meal you don't intend to eat. And all you can think about is the mess.* Supper used to be a time when we would sit and talk about our day. James would cook and Mom and I would do the dishes, the whole time talking about nothing and everything.

"And if you could, please…" Mom hesitated, but the familiar look and the circular motion of her finger around her own face spoke volumes before she even said the words "…wash your face?"

"That's okay, Mom. I'll just stay in my room," I said acidly. "Can't have your daughter making a bad impression."

She looked relieved. "Thanks, dear."

"Whatever. There's mail for you." I pointed at the pile on the kitchen table.

Mom picked up the little white envelope on top and stared at it. Her face dropped and the excitement of her pending night out vanished. "Where did you get this?"

"In the mail." *I just said that.* I stopped cleaning and leaned against the counter, watching Mom.

She quickly turned the envelope over and examined it. "You didn't open it did you?" She was shaking.

"Of course not. Jeeze, Mom, calm down. Who's it from?"

"None of your damn business, that's who." She stormed from the room, taking the card with her.

Woah. I shook my head and went back to wiping the counter. What kind of mail could set Mom off like that?

As promised, I was in my room with all evidence of cooking cleaned up when the ladies arrived an hour later. I was hurt that Mom didn't want to introduce me. I peered out of my room to see her friends. Mom hadn't had anyone over to the house for a long time and I was curious. Maybe she was finally getting over James. A girl could hope, couldn't she? Three women including Mom were in the living room chatting.

One lady stood and studied the picture of Queen Elizabeth and Prince Philip. She looked around the room like she was searching for something. "Julia, wasn't there a beautiful painting of a sunset here?"

I strained to hear Mom's answer. She hated to talk about James, and I wondered what she would say.

"Yeah. I got rid of it. I was tired of the painting." She smiled as she looked up at the picture. "I love the royals. Don't you?"

"I can take 'em or leave 'em," said the lady eyeing the print.

"I'd rather have a painting," the third lady said.

"Well. Not me," said Mom tersely. "James is gone and so are his paintings."

"What did Victoria say about it?"

"She's too young to understand." Mom placed her hands on her hips and raised her chin. She seemed so certain, it was all I could do to stay quiet. I wasn't too young to have an opinion; she just never asked for it or considered how I felt. By the time I had gotten home the day James left, the damage was done. I wanted to tell her so, but I stayed back.

"Victoria thinks she wants to paint, but I'm not having it," Mom continued. "When James was painting he got so caught up in it...I used to feel so ignored and alone." She paused. "There's no way I'm going to be abandoned by my daughter too."

The other two didn't argue but they shared a glance that said they weren't sure about her reasoning. *Neither am I, ladies.* I slipped back into my room, mad that Mom didn't want me painting, and hurt that she was ashamed of the way I looked. I just didn't want to look like everyone else. Was that really so bad?

I grabbed my sketchbook and opened it. A quick sketch I'd

made of Zach stared back. *You can keep me in my room, hidden from your friends,* I thought, *but you can't keep me from painting.*

I flopped on my bed and closed my eyes. With a deep breath, I pushed away the thoughts of Mom and concentrated on Zach. I thought of his beautiful ocean-coloured eyes and strong body. I imagined what it would be like to go on a date with him. As I drifted off to sleep, I kept replaying the scene where he said to come early on Saturday so we could talk.

I dreamt of Zach. We were hanging out, eating pizza at Tomaso's. We talked and laughed until midnight. Then we grabbed some paint and created the most amazing picture on the side of the pizza shop. It was so good the owner decided to make it permanent. He offered us free pizza and pop for life. Everything was going along great until Officer Mitchell showed up and handed me the white envelope with the card inside. This time it was addressed to me. I opened it and all it said was "It's time for the truth."

I woke up in a sweat. I checked my phone. It was seven o'clock. Mom would already be gone to work, so I crawled out of bed and tiptoed down the hall to her room. My stomach began to knot. I shouldn't be doing this, but I had to know. I searched the top of her bureau and in the drawers. Nothing. I looked on the bookshelf and in the closet. Finally, I opened the small drawer of her nightstand. There it was. I grabbed the small white envelope, rushed back to my room, shoved it in my backpack, and got ready for school before I could change my mind.

I stumbled through the morning and made my way to the cafeteria at lunch. I was looking forward to finding Justine and having someone to talk to.

"Hey." I sat down with my sandwich. "Can I tell you something?"

"Sure," said Justine. She put her fork down and took out both of her ear buds.

"Yesterday, there was a card in the mail for my mom. She got really upset when she saw it. And when I asked where it came from she yelled for me to mind my own business and stomped out of the room. She wouldn't discuss it. It made me curious so...I stole the card."

"You did *what*?" Justine's mouth hung open.

"I needed to see why it made her so angry. But I haven't had the guts to open it yet."

"Maybe it's from some old boyfriend or something," Justine suggested, picking up her fork.

I took a couple of bites of sandwich, considering the possibility. I thought of James. "Hmm, I don't think so. I think it's more serious. She wasn't just angry...she was almost afraid?"

Justine shrugged.

"Doesn't make any sense," I said.

"Not everything makes sense." Justine sighed. "Like algebra."

"Trouble with math?"

Justine made a face. "Math *is* the trouble."

"Let me see it. Maybe I can help." I moved my tray to the side and Justine pulled out her textbook. We spent the rest of lunch working through her homework.

"Oh my God, thank you so much," Justine said gratefully as she stuffed her book back in her bag, flung it over her shoulder, and grabbed her tray.

"No problem." *Math questions are easy to solve.* I waved and headed to next period.

Mr. Fawthrope was reading from *Romeo and Juliet* today. Usually I liked Shakespeare and the old language he used. Other kids seem to think it was hard, but I actually enjoyed the challenge. Today I didn't care. The card seemed to be singing to me from my backpack; a background hum that was getting harder and harder to ignore. Did I really want to open it?

Mr. Fawthrope called my name and I jumped.

Kate giggled.

I glared at her and then looked back to Mr. Fawthrope. "Sorry. Rough night."

Mr. Fawthrope looked at me. He seemed concerned. He nodded and continued on with the story.

"Out too late doing your fancy art?" whispered Mark.

"Nah, she's part of a 'project' now," answered Jeremy. The way he said "project" made it sound like I had been quarantined.

I didn't comment. I had other things to think about. I had just decided I was going to open the card. If Romeo and Juliet could die for love, I could open a silly envelope.

TEN

I took off as soon as the bell rang. I didn't want an audience. I sat down on the bench behind the school where some students had planted a small flower garden. Yellow daffodils burst free from their green buds, velvety red tulips swayed gently in the breeze, purple and white crocuses opened and closed with the rise and fall of the sun. Each spring the flowers returned, sharing their determination to survive even the harshest of winters.

I took the envelope from my backpack and stared at it. I took a deep breath, held it for a few seconds, and blew it out. I turned the envelope over and over. Finally, I tore it open and pulled out the card. I could not believe what I read.

Dear Julia,
I just wanted to let you know that Richard is not well. It may be terminal. If Victoria wants to meet her father, she needs to do it now. He is staying with me as long as he can, then he will go to the hospital.
Please, Julia, time is of the essence.
Love, Elsie

I read it again and again.
Richard.
Father.
My heart pounded, making my chest hurt. The yellow, red, purple, and white of the flowers began to swirl together. How could I have a father who was alive? I had *just* asked Mom about him. She said he was dead. Like she always did. And she was angry that I had even asked.

He wasn't dead. That was good, wasn't it? But he hadn't contacted me in fifteen years. That was bad. I sat there, stunned. Suddenly, bile rose in my throat and I turned and puked on the tulips.

Why would Mom lie to me? I was confused, but felt certain about one thing: there was no way I was going to risk the pain of being hurt by another parent. I would *not* meet this Richard guy. But I would definitely confront Mom. My shock was slowly solidifying into anger. I'd do it now. I left the school and headed downtown.

I never went in to Mom's work, but today was different. I walked the length of Halifax in record time, anger fuelling each step. I wouldn't let Mom stomp out of this conversation.

I arrived at the IWK and headed straight for the nurses' desk on the third floor. I was about to demand to see Julia Markham when I caught a glimpse of her in a room caring for a little boy. I watched. She stroked his hair and touched his cheek gently. She smiled at him and laughed when he laughed. She spoke softly and began to read from a storybook as he pointed at the pictures. She was being so thoughtful and tender it was more than I could bear.

I remembered her reading to me when I was little — I had loved fairy tales best. We'd snuggle on my bed, and pull my fluffy comforter all the way up to my chin. My hair would still be wet from the bath, the smell of strawberry shampoo still fresh. Mom would read with great enthusiasm, giving each character a different voice. Even though we read each book dozens of times, each reading always felt magical and new. I was warm and safe. Happy. Now, all she did was find fault with everything I did. If she could love a complete stranger, why couldn't she love me?

My heart ached as my hot anger quickly snuffed to cold self-doubt. Confronting Mom at work would only lead to a freak-out. She'd have to admit to her co-workers that the strange goth girl was her daughter, and that would make her even more angry. Then she'd get mad because I'd taken the card. Everything would be my fault....

Coming here was a bad idea. The triage nurse was eyeing me, so I raced for the elevator and pounded the down button once, twice, three times.

"Come on, come on!" I coaxed, but it wasn't coming fast enough.

I flung myself through the door for the stairwell instead. When the door clanged shut behind me, the silence enveloped me and I bent over and put my hands on my knees. All of a sudden, I couldn't catch my breath and tears were prickling my eyes. I sat on the step and sobbed.

Eventually the tears stopped. I felt drained, empty, almost hollow. My feet were like lead as I trudged home.

Once in my room I looked at the card again. *Love, Elsie.* I wracked my brain. That name...that was Richard's mother, so... she must be...my grandmother. Why had I never met her? Why hadn't I pushed Mom to know more all these years? But I knew the answer to that: I used to be so eager to please her that I never would've asked a question that might upset her. Now it didn't matter if I asked or not. Upsetting her just seemed to come naturally to me these days.

I glanced back down at the card. There was an email address included at the bottom. I wasn't ready to meet Richard, but maybe I could message Elsie.

I sat in front of the computer in our living room without turning it on. I stared at a little picture in a homemade frame on the desk beside the monitor. It was one I had made for Mother's Day years ago. Mom used to always make a big deal about my creative side, covering the fridge with my artwork, buying me new crayons.

I finally pushed the power button and waited for the screen to light up. I knew Mom's password because I had helped her set up her account. When I began to enter Elsie's email address, the rest of it auto-filled. That meant the address was already in the contacts. I checked the sent folder and found an email Mom had sent to the same address:

Please stop trying to contact me. I have made up my mind, and Victoria is not going to meet Richard.

Maybe Mom thought I didn't need to meet my family. But she hadn't bothered to ask me.

I stared at the screen. What do you say to some lady who may or may not be the grandmother you didn't know you had? I typed, deleted, and retyped three times. In the end, it was short and to the point:

Dear Elsie,
I found the card. It's me, Vic (Victoria). I'd like to meet you. Don't tell Julia. Call me at home between 7 and 7:30 A.M.
Vic

I hit send before I could reconsider.

When Mom got home I was in my room reading and I planned on staying there.

"Victoria," she sang. "I'm home." Her voice was light, happy. *Cool. I don't care.*

"Come into the kitchen."

I threw my book down and got up. I traipsed to the kitchen. Mom smiled. "I bought some fish, and stuff for a salad. Doesn't that sound good?"

"Yeah," I muttered. I really wasn't hungry.

"Do you want it pan-fried or baked?" Mom took the salmon from the package and began to season it.

"Whatever."

"I know I don't do a lot of the cooking, so I thought I'd treat you."

No comment.

"I think I'll bake the fish. Could you cut up some lettuce and tomatoes?"

I slammed the cutting board on the counter and angrily chopped at head of Romaine. I practically pulverized the tomato.

Mom looked over at me. "Is something the matter, Victoria?"

"Nope. Everything's perfect." I scooped up the chopped vegetables and dropped them in a bowl. I plunked the bowl on the table.

"Are you sure? You seem upset. Did something happen at school today?"

I did not want to have this conversation. Not yet, it was still too raw and I was too tired to fight. "Yeah. That's it. But don't worry. I can handle it." I turned to leave. "I'm going to go back to my room."

"Okay. I'll call you when the fish is ready."

"Can't wait." I stomped away.

We ate in silence. Mom didn't ask me again about being upset and I didn't offer to tell her any more.

I went to bed early but didn't sleep well. I tossed and turned. The bright numbers on my digital clock mocked me — 1:00 A.M.: "it's really late, you better get some sleep"; 3:00 A.M.: "ha, ha, you're still awake"; 5:00 A.M.: "forget it; it's almost time to get up." When my alarm buzzed at 6 it was a relief to get out of bed, even though I was still exhausted. I hurried to get dressed and apply my Goth Girl makeup. I didn't want to miss Elsie when she called.

But the phone didn't ring. I couldn't believe it.

This lady had tried to make contact first, and now she was rejecting me, too. Did *anyone* give a damn about me? I left for school, slamming the door behind me.

There was no call on Friday, either. I wracked my brain, trying to justify the delay. *Not everyone checks their email every day.* The voice in my head was firm and reasonable. *Maybe she'll call tomorrow.* But tomorrow is Saturday and Mom will be home.

Then it struck me. With all the card drama I had let it slip my mind: *Tomorrow is Saturday and I get to see Zach.* My inner voice was suddenly much more pleasant as I daydreamed about what might happen with Zach. I reached for my sketchpad. My mind was racing, and it felt good to translate that frantic energy into sketches.

Zach bled into everything I drew: the guards at Citadel Hill all had his jawline. The log cabin had a candle-lit table set for two. The fancy condominium came with a muscular salesman that stood with his thumbs in his pockets.

Forget Mom, Richard, and Elsie.

After all, they'd forgotten me.

ELEVEN

Saturday. It was grey and drizzly but thoughts of Zach made me feel sunny and warm. I had replaced the card in Mom's drawer before she realized it was gone, and thoughts of Elsie and Richard were tucked away and replaced with images of a certain badass guy that wanted to talk to me. I should have given him my number last week so we could have texted a bit. I rushed out of the house and set off for the art group. I was psyched to see Zach, but today was also the day we'd finally get to see the fence we were going to paint.

When I neared the office building I saw Zach leaning against the brick outside the glass doors. He was turned away from me, but I knew it was him by the way he stood with his hands in his pockets.

I called out. He turned and waved. My stomach flipped.

"Hey," he said when I reached him. He stood close. "Let's get out of here. This art project is lame." He gave me a killer smile and stepped a little closer. "We could head to over to the mall and get something to eat."

I was tempted, but I had these ideas about the project I wanted to share. I had been drawing in my sketchpad and on every scrap of paper or notebook I could find. I felt torn, which surprised me.

Zach noticed my hesitation. "Jeeze, Vic. You actually want to spend time with these whiners?" He placed a warm hand on my shoulder, his eyes pleaded.

My knees went weak and I'm sure my heart skipped a beat. "Of course not," I scoffed. I backed away slightly so his hand fell from my shoulder, allowing me to breathe again. I looked up and down the sidewalk for a distraction, but there was nothing but beige concrete. "But we're supposed to get the chance to go to the construction site today. Aren't you the least bit curious?" I remembered the keen look in his eyes when he had looked at the artwork on the screen that first day, and the way he had sat straight up, focused.

"Look. We helped with ideas last week, so we know what's gonna end up on the wall." He ran his fingers through his hair and grinned at me. "Come on. They won't miss us for one week."

"I don't know. What if Russell or Peter screws up my good idea?"

"So, you'll fix it later." Zach kept looking at me, and I could feel myself starting to cave. My pulse quickened when I thought about spending time with just him, forgetting everything else.

"Don't you like to paint?" I asked in a last-ditch effort to stay.

"Yeah, but having to do what I'm told drives me nuts. I am a man of free will — an independent thinker."

"Right. So how did all that independent thinking lead to this?" I gestured at the building.

"Well, I got nabbed doing some graffiti at school. My penalty was supposed to be more severe because I've been caught three times now, but my dad knows a local judge and he pulled some strings."

"Oh yeah, that's totally fair." I rolled my eyes and threw him a mocking smile. "Only a little rich boy could get away with being a repeat offender."

"Hey." Zach pushed my shoulder, gently, pretending to be insulted.

I shrugged and stuck my tongue out, laughing. "I know what you mean about being told what to do, though. I hate that they're telling us where and when to paint."

"Yeah. I don't think they get that what makes art good is that it's inspired, not forced."

I knew it, he really does get it. He isn't just a jock.

"So what were you painting when you got caught?"

"Mostly just some dumb tags." He kicked at a crack in the sidewalk, hands in his pockets. "Then I painted this pic of our principal looking like a tyrant ruling his kingdom of kids, who were all in chains."

I was impressed. "No way. I bet that didn't go over well."

"Yeah, Dad really had to extend some favours to get me here." Zach rubbed his thumb against his index finger indicating there might have been money involved. He laughed hollowly.

"The luxury of money, I guess. But it's not all bad: you got to meet me." I looked right into his eyes, hoping the bold line would land.

"That's right, Vic," he said seriously. "Art has brought us together; it's our destiny." Zach waved his arms like he was giving a grand speech, convincing the world that what he said was true. "If we hadn't been out defacing public property, I wouldn't know you." He stopped waving his arms around and looked at me. "I think it's a good thing we both bend the rules."

I laughed. "I'm not sure anyone else would agree with that, but I'm glad we met."

Zach smiled, and I felt warm despite the drizzle.

"Come on. Let's go." Zach reached for my hand.

We took off down the street. My heart pounded in my ears and my stomach filled with excitement. Zach's grip on my fingers urged me on. I glanced back once and saw the other delinquents beginning to arrive. Zach and I rounded the corner, out of sight, and stopped to catch our breath. I let go of his hand and leaned over, gasping and laughing at the same time.

Standing straight again, I noticed the sparkle in Zach's eyes, his cheeks flushed from running. "We did it!" I hooted.

But my excitement was short-lived.

"Where are you two off to in such a hurry?" asked a familiar male voice from behind me.

"*Shit*," I muttered. This time I turned around before I was asked. "Hey, Officer Mitchell. Um, Zach and I were just having a little race."

"Yeah. Well, let's see who can get back to the rest of the group first." He jerked his thumb back toward the group assembled at the front doors of the building.

I started walking back, but Zach didn't move. I stopped and watched Officer Mitchell stride over to Zach and place his hand gently on Zach's shoulder, as if to coax him.

Zach jerked away. "Hands off," he snarled. He gave the cop a filthy look.

"Just go back to the group."

Reluctantly, Zach complied.

We made our way back to the group. We didn't speak, but Zach gave me a flash of his cocky smile and I knew he was feeling the same rush of adrenaline I was. If we'd been just a few seconds faster, we would have made it.

Officer Mitchell walked behind us the whole way, making sure we didn't take another detour. He was pissed, but I didn't care.

Cathy was the first to speak when we got to the group. "Hello, Vic," she said. "Are you ready to see where you'll be painting?"

I nodded.

"Good morning, Zach," Cathy continued brightly. "Glad

you decided to come with us. I know your dad will be happy you did." She leaned in and said a little quieter: "This is your last chance."

"Whatever," grumbled Zach as he pushed by her and leaned on the wall by the glass doors. He took out his sunglasses and put them on despite the clouds.

"Hey, what's up, Vic?" asked Russell. "Did the jock and the girl-in-black think they were getting out of the group today?"

"That's not a very nice way to play with your new friends, is it?" Peter snorted and gave Russell a fist bump.

"Shut up," I snapped.

"Relax." Peter rolled his eyes. "We're just here to make art." He shifted his weight from one foot to the other.

"Yeah," said Russell. "Bring it on!" He jumped to meet Peter and gave him a high-five. His shoulder-length curls bounced.

"Okay, guys, we aren't going into the building today, we are going down the street a couple of blocks to where we'll be painting." Cathy gestured with her hand to show which direction we would be heading.

We followed obediently.

"I hope the rain holds off so we can get to work." Cathy spoke as we walked to a corner where there used to be a gas station. Now there was a construction site surrounded by a large plywood fence.

Rachael sidled up to Zach on the short walk. "Hi, Zach," she cooed. "I thought you weren't going to make it today, and I was so sad." She pouted like a two year old. "This project really needs your strong muscles and great ideas." She winked at him and smiled like an idiot.

I pretended to stick a finger down my throat and gag.

Russell and Peter hooted with laughter.

Rachael quelled them in an instant. "You're not laughing at me, are you, boys?" she asked with saccharine sweetness.

Both punks stopped immediately. "No, no." Russell cleared his throat, stood up straight, and wiped the grin from his face.

"Russell just told me a great joke." Peter nodded.

"We'd never laugh at you," said Russell, walking over and putting a hand on Rachael's back.

"Okay," she giggled.

I shook my head. I was grateful Cathy spoke before I had to witness any more of Rachael's drama; I was afraid I'd puke.

"So! This is the spot for our mural," Cathy explained. "You'll use chalk to rough in the images you sketched out last week. That way, it's easier to make changes as you work. Once you're all satisfied, we'll bring out the paint."

I began transferring my ideas onto the wood panels. The conversation stopped as we all worked. I looked up and down the length of the fence. We were spaced evenly along the way with each artist claiming four panels. We had divided up the work and agreed to each start on a different section. Eventually, we would overlap and combine our styles along the length of the whole mural.

We worked away; Cathy and Officer Mitchell supervised and chatted. Occasionally, the sun tried to peek out from behind the clouds and I tried to covertly check Zach out every once in a while. Sometimes he'd catch me looking and wink. Most of the time, though, he was so engrossed in the work he didn't even notice.

Cathy's voice startled me. "Before we end for the day, there are a few places we have to go to clean up some tags and misplaced art. They're all in the north end. We'll be travelling in two cars: mine and the police cruiser."

Zach groaned.

"That's right. It's not all fun and games." Officer Mitchell spoke with his "I mean business" voice. He motioned for Zach to get into his car. I followed, as Russell, Peter, and Rachael got in with Cathy.

My second trip in Officer Mitchell's squad car was different than the first. I gladly hopped in the back seat next to Zach. The disgusting odours that had assaulted my nostrils last time were hidden by the delicious spicy smell of his body spray.

"So, have you ever been in a police car before?" Zach asked after the doors were shut and we were moving.

"Yup. This very one." I nodded. "How about you?"

"Yeah. A couple of times. But the third time I got caught, they called my dad and he came and picked me up." He looked out the window. "I liked the cruiser better."

"How is a cop car better?"

"It's not the car, it's the company." He smiled and reached for my hand. He gently rubbed his thumb on the back of my hand, almost like he was sketching something there. My skin tingled where he touched it. "Hey, speaking of cars, I got my license a couple of weeks ago. My dad agreed to get me some wheels if I stop doing graffiti."

Wow. A dad and a car. Lucky guy. "Thanks for the warning," I teased. "I'll be safe on the sidewalk, right?"

"Not to worry. Next week I'll pick you up and you won't have to use the sidewalk."

My stomach did a flip, but I managed to keep my cool. "Sure."

We traded phone numbers and I gave him my address. I saw Officer Mitchell's reflection in the rear-view mirror. There was disapproval in his eyes, but that actually made me feel even better. *What do you know?* I sank back in the seat. My mind yo-yoed between the present conversation with Zach and the possibility of being alone with him next week. It occurred to me that the only problem with the ride in the police car this time was that it was too short.

The first and second stops were both on Gottingen Street. Most of the tags we had to remove were just basic and lame; it actually felt good to cover them with fresh, clean paint. Tagging had been my first foray into "public art," but I was always secretly glad whenever my tags got removed. They weren't really that good, and it was as if the city clean-up crew were my personal human erasers. Now, I was painting full pictures and they weren't half bad — seeing *those* patched stung.

The last stop was too familiar. I got out of the cruiser and stood staring as the vibrations of the traffic overhead shook me to the core. My favourite spot now reminded me of all the things going on with my so-called family. It was no longer easier to breathe here. My emotions and thoughts about the card and Mom started bubbling to the surface. I took a shaky breath, pushing them back down.

"Wow, this one's good." Russell eyed the painted concrete in front of him.

"Yeah, do we really have to paint over this?" Peter asked Cathy.

"Sorry, but yes we do. It's here illegally and has to go." Cathy turned to me.

My throat got dry and my eyes began to sting. *Get it together, Goth Girl.* I swallowed hard, threw my shoulders back, and raised my chin. I wasn't ready to admit it was my work. There was a reason I painted at night, alone, in the dark. My bravery faded in the sun. I picked up a roller and headed toward the stone wall.

I felt a hand on my shoulder. I turned around.

"Bold colours, heavy lines." Zach raised his eyebrows and tilted his head toward the picture. He spoke softly so the others wouldn't hear him repeat the words I had said to him the first time we spoke. "Is this yours?"

I wanted to lie but I couldn't. I nodded.

"It's great." He reached down and gently squeezed my hand. "Most of the stuff I painted was just to piss people off, but this...." He paused and took in the colours. "This is real art, Vic."

The cartoon image depicted an ugly green queen perched on

her throne, high on a mountaintop. Struggling up the side of the rock was a girl in a bright pink shirt, her blue jeans torn, her face scraped, and her fingers bloody. She was dodging falling rocks, thorny branches, and lightning bolts as the queen looked down, mocking her efforts. The colours were bold and bright. In the lower right-hand corner the bubble-letter tag read "Goth Girl."

"Thanks." I managed. My hand sizzled with heat.

"You are an amazing artist." Zach stared at the piece.

"You're smarter than I thought." I pretended to punch him in the shoulder, blowing off the true feelings in my gut. It felt good to have him call me an artist. I wanted people to like what I did. And if another artist was the one giving the compliment, that was even better.

Zach laughed and put his arm around me.

Rachael noticed. "Hey, you two!" she called. "Get over here and get to work. Come on, Zach." Rachael offered her hand to Zach. "There's room right here." She winked and flashed her dumb smile.

Zach made his way over but chose a spot between Russell and Peter.

"Goth Girl?" asked Rachael. "That someone you know, Vic?" She turned to me.

"Never heard of her," I replied. "You think just because I look like this I know everyone who dresses goth?" My voice was louder than I wanted.

"Jeeze, calm down," said Russell.

"I suppose you know every dumb blonde, then?" I continued barking at Rachael. I knew I was blowing my cover, but I couldn't help myself. I felt angry and hurt, watching my work disappear. I had been secretly hoping my art, because it was good, would be allowed to stay.

Rachael just huffed and turned away.

The first stroke of paint made me feel sick. I bit my lip so hard it started to bleed. The physical pain was better than the ache in my heart. I began moving my roller faster and faster. I just wanted to be done.

When the session was finally over, I was exhausted but I wasn't quite ready to say goodbye to Zach. I wanted to spend some more time with him, but his dad had pulled up in a shiny SUV. He was wearing a suit and tie. He didn't look happy.

"That's my ride. See ya next week." Zach waved as he slid into the car.

I watched him go, wishing he could stay.

Twelve

The closer I got to home the slower I walked. I had managed to keep the idea of having a father — a dying father — and a grandmother out of my mind when I was busy sketching, painting, and talking. But now. Alone. I paused on the front doorstep. I could no longer deny my curiosity about the contents of the card.

I took a deep breath and entered the house. I checked the answering machine. No messages. I sat in front of the computer and turned it on. No emails. *Man! What's up with this family?* I hit the power button hard enough to shake the desk, knocking over the framed Mother's Day picture. I left it.

Why hadn't Elsie called or emailed? Weren't grandmothers supposed to be kind and loving and bake cookies? And weren't dads supposed to teach you to play catch and help you with homework? And get you out of trouble like Zach's dad? I grabbed my phone and texted him: "Hey."

His reply was instant. "Hey yourself."

I smiled and sank into the couch as I sent the next message. An hour later I heard the door open and rushed up to my room. I didn't want to talk to Mom just yet. And screw having a dad. I'd made it fifteen years without one. It was his loss.

At lunch on Monday, Justine asked about the card. "So did you open it?"

"Yeah. Get this: it was about my *father*. Apparently I still have one." Even saying the words out loud felt strange. "But I've decided I don't care." I tried to sound convincing.

"Your dad is alive?" Justine asked, her eyebrows raised in shock.

"Yeah, but he hasn't bothered to contact me, so I'm not going to bother with him. I have all I need without him and his mother."

"Woah. Your grandmother?"

"Mhmm. The card was from her. She was trying to convince Mom to get me to meet Richard because he's sick and might be dying or something." I pushed my fries around on the tray. "Whatever, I say: so long *Dad*."

"Really?" Justine eyes grew big with disbelief. "My dad had a mild heart attack last year and it was awful."

"Really," I said, but the word stuck in my throat and came out way too high. I slumped in my seat.

Justine stared at me for a minute. Then she nodded and changed the subject. "So, tell me about the rich boy then."

I immediately sat up and began rambling. I told Justine about Zach and me trying to take off from the group and Officer Mitchell bringing us back. I told her about riding in the cop car with Zach, how good he smelled, and how easy it was to talk with him.

"*And* he's going to pick me up on Saturday." My smile was wide and I probably looked like a fool, but I didn't care.

"Good thing you don't like him, then, huh?" Justine laughed.

The conversation lulled as we both ate. I didn't mind. My thoughts drifted to Zach.

Justine interrupted my daydreaming.

"Hey, want to know a funny story?"

I looked back at her and smiled. "Always."

"Yesterday, my little brother climbed this huge tree in our backyard." A grin grew on her face as she spoke. "He said he planned on scaring me when I got home from work."

I nodded, letting her know I was listening.

"But the joke was on him. He climbed too high, spooked himself, and got stuck. We had to wait for my older brother to get home and help him out of the tree."

We laughed as we gathered up our trays and books.

I entered English class. Mr. Fawthrope motioned for me to approach his desk. "How are things going, Victoria?" he asked. "You seemed upset the other day."

"Fine."

"Glad to hear that. But if you ever need someone to talk to, I'm here."

"Sure thing." I liked Mr. Fawthrope, but I wasn't about to tell him about my family and all their troubles. I walked away and slid into my chair.

"Have a seat, everybody," he called, "and get ready for today's test."

What? I'd forgotten all about the test. I hadn't even finished the book I was supposed to read. I'd never forgotten a test in my life. *Shit.* Panic pounded in my chest.

When the papers were handed out I stared at the white sheet. I read the questions twice: How does the author use setting as conflict? Give two examples of symbolism from the novel. How does the protagonist change throughout the novel? I had no idea how to answer any of them.

I glanced quickly around the room. Everyone had their heads down, pens scratching across paper. Obviously, I was the only one unprepared. I leaned forward and sighed. I sat back up and looked at Kate, who sat directly to my left. Kate looked up for a second and noticed my blank paper. She smiled slightly, then returned to her writing, moving one hand along furiously and using the other to cover her work.

Thanks for the help. Not that I would cheat anyway. I'd never done that before, either. I tried to conjure answers to the questions. I knew they weren't correct, but sitting there doing nothing was unbearable — and something I'd never really experienced before. The clock slowly ticked by. The bell finally relieved me of my torture. I handed the paper to Mr. Fawthrope, but I couldn't look him in the eye.

"Sorry," I said as I ran out of the room.

The rest of the school week was a blur and work was awful.

"Victoria, I thought I asked you to fill the cooler?" Mr. Habib motioned to the empty shelves where the milk should be.

"Right. Yes. Sorry, I forgot. I'll do it right now." I rushed to the stock room and tripped over a box of cans waiting to be put away.

"Damn," I muttered as I reached for the rolling cans.

"Victoria?" Mr. Habib came around the corner to investigate the noise. "Are you okay?"

"I'm fine." I picked up the cans quickly and stuffed them back in the cardboard box. As I made my way to the cooler with the milk, I looked up at the clock. *Please let this shift be over soon.*

Whenever I could, I texted Zach. If he didn't reply right away, I'd scroll through the old texts and re-read them. I kept picturing him and remembered the way his hand felt on mine in the back of the police car.

I had gotten good at avoiding Mom, claiming I had lots of homework. And she didn't seek me out. I guess we finally had something in common: neither of us wanted to talk about Elsie or Richard. But not talking wasn't working either. I wanted to confront Mom and scream at her, but I didn't have the guts. I wasn't sure I wanted to know the truth. Why had she lied? Why didn't the man who was my father insist on seeing me?

When Saturday morning finally rolled around and Mom was still sitting in the kitchen I started to get antsy. I didn't want her here when Zach showed up.

"Don't you have errands to run?" I tried to sound nonchalant.

"Yeah. I'm just finishing my tea. There's no rush." She looked up at me and narrowed her eyes. "Are you trying to get rid of me for some reason?"

"No. No. I know you don't like the grocery store when it's too busy, that's all." I fumbled around the kitchen. *God, would you just leave already?*

"Did you want me to drive you to the art project?" Mom glanced at her watch.

"No." I answered too quickly and Mom looked at me with a puzzled look. "I...I still need to shower. And put on my makeup."

Mom grimaced. "Of course, you wouldn't want to go anywhere without the makeup." She stood up and placed her teacup in the sink.

I left the room and headed for the bathroom, ignoring the anger in my gut. I stood in the shower, letting the hot water and steam relax the tension in my shoulders. I lathered the shampoo and rinsed.

As I stepped out of the shower, I could hear Mom still moving around downstairs. I prayed she would leave soon — Zach was supposed to be here in twenty minutes. I wrapped myself in a towel and headed to the kitchen. I had to find a way to get Mom to leave, but when I passed the little hall table where she always put her purse, it was already gone.

I heard another noise and started to panic. If Mom was gone, who was here?

Not only did I not have my Goth Girl makeup, I didn't even have clothes on. How could I defend myself from an attacker while wearing just a towel?

I pressed myself to the wall and edged my way toward the kitchen. Maybe I could get a look, see how big this person was, and figure out what I was up against.

I craned my neck and peeked around the corner.

"Zach!" I shouted.

I was relieved he wasn't an attacker, but my relief quickly turned back to a different kind of panic: he was way too early. I wasn't ready.

He was staring at me with an odd expression. I backed away. His eyes made me cross my arms and look at the floor.

"No, don't go." Zach moved toward me.

"B-but I'm not dressed," I stammered. "I just got out of the shower. I don't have any makeup on or anything."

"I know," he said softly. "You're gorgeous." Zach closed the gap between us and took me in his arms.

I froze. Then I relaxed against him and took a deep breath. The familiar spicy scent of his body spray filled my nose and his chest was hard and warm. I didn't want to move.

He looked down at me and then gently raised my chin toward his. I looked into his eyes and he stared back, his eyes smouldering with intensity. I was thrilled and a bit unnerved at the same time. I swallowed. He lowered his head, one hand on each side of my face, and kissed my eyes, then the tip of my nose. His kisses were soft and light like fresh snowflakes falling on my face — tingling before they were gone.

My heart raced and I held by breath. Finally, his lips met mine.

Then his cellphone rang.

"It's my dad," groaned Zach. "I gotta get this. He's pissed that I tried to skip out on the group last week, so he's making sure I get there this time."

"It's okay." I stepped back. I wasn't used to this new sensation and I wasn't sure I was even ready for it. I rushed back upstairs to get dressed.

I could still feel the touch of his mouth on mine. I almost poked myself in the eye trying to put on my makeup. I needed the eyeliner and mascara more than ever right now. Dressed in my familiar black, I sighed out loud. *There, that's better. Safer. Hidden.* I slowly walked back to the living room where Zach was eyeing the picture over the couch.

"Someone likes the royal family," he said.

"Yeah. A bit too much, if you ask me."

"It's kind of creepy."

"I know, right?"

"Hey," said Zach. He pouted. "You got dressed."

The back of my knees tingled at the look on his face. What would have happened if his phone hadn't gone off? I was kind of glad I'd never know — but also kind of disappointed.

"Yeah. If not, we'd be late." I reached for my phone and tucked it in my pocket. "Let's get going." I turned to leave the living room, heading back toward the kitchen, but stopped when Zach didn't follow.

"Yeah, guess we better go. Dad is keeping pretty tight reins on me right now," said Zach. But he still didn't make any move to go. He put out his hand and I moved closer to him.

"At least you have a dad." I pushed the thought of my own father from my mind. I still hadn't heard a word from him or Elsie. But I wasn't going to let some absent father spoil this.

"Just because he's there, doesn't make him a good father." Zach looked away for a second, and then sighed. "My dad likes to throw around money and buy me stuff, but he doesn't actually care about me...as long as I don't interfere with his world. Right now he's interested because he stuck his neck out for me and I'm making him look bad. Once this settles down, he won't give me the time of day." Zach leaned forward and kissed me on the cheek. "Money's not the only thing he likes to throw around, either."

I searched his eyes. "What do you mean?"

Zach shrugged. "Sometimes he gets really angry and throws a couple of punches my way."

I began to say something, but Zach kissed my mouth, making my words disappear. He pulled back, tucked a strand of hair behind my left ear, and smiled.

"Forget it. That's why I go to the gym. I work out to stay strong. He doesn't hurt me, and I make sure he doesn't go near my little sister." Again, he kissed me. I leaned in to him and twisted my fingers into his hair. "We better get going or we might not make it to the mural." His voice was low and raspy.

I tried to catch my breath and ignore my racing heart and tingling lips. "I think you're right." I broke free from his hold and moved toward the kitchen and the door. I was sure if we stayed a second longer I'd never let go.

He took my hand again and led me outside where his green sedan was parked.

"So, this is your new car?"

He opened the door for me and I hopped in, smiling like a princess.

"Yeah. It's second-hand, but at least it's mine. I wanted a Mustang, but Dad said I'd have to settle for this Camry for now."

I figured it would be a long time before I had *any* car. I sighed and let my thoughts drift to the painting we were approaching. We were meeting the others at the construction site.

"So what do you think about the mural?"

"It's okay," Zach replied. "Not really my thing."

"Yeah, but the early-village scene with the log cabins that Peter is working on is pretty cool."

"True. And Russell has a knack for lettering." Zach stopped for a red light and looked over at me. "Your stuff's great too." Zach raised his eyebrows and ogled me.

I made a funny face back, but my heart skipped a beat.

"Really, though," he said, accelerating, "I like your cartooning. It makes the skyscraper you're working on look like it's twenty years in the future."

"Thanks." I beamed with pride. "What's your favourite style?"

"Actually, I'd rather do charcoal sketches." Zach sighed. "I took up graffiti to piss off my dad. It's hard to get in trouble with a piece of charcoal." He chuckled.

"I never really thought of getting into trouble, even though I knew it was against the law. I just love the look of street art." I thought of the excitement of graffiti and the joy of being creative. "I was watching this show and they were showing some great pieces in New York and stuff by Banksy. I just thought, *I can do that*. It kind of reminds me of tattooing, but larger... and less painful."

Zach nodded. "I have a tattoo, but it's not great. It was another one of my ideas to tick off my dad."

"Do you ever do anything that doesn't make your father angry?" I studied Zach's face.

"Sometimes. When he gets really mad, then I do whatever it takes to please him for a bit. Like going to this art project." Zach looked at me sideways and smirked.

Is that what I'm doing? I wondered. Sneaking out, doing graffiti — was it just to get Mom's attention? *Maybe in the beginning, but not anymore. Now, the art itself keeps me going.*

"So, I know you don't want to do *this* art project, but what would you like to do? What kind of charcoal sketches?" I asked.

"I'd like to draw a picture of you." He reached over and placed a hand on my thigh.

The thought of Zach taking the time to draw me made me blush. His hand was warm on my leg. "Me? Why?"

"Because you're beautiful," he said simply. "And I want to sketch you just the way I saw you this morning."

"You're crazy." I circled my finger around the side of my head.

"Crazy about you."

My legs turned to jelly.

As soon as Zach parked, I opened the door. The cool air was refreshing. I tested my legs; I wasn't completely sure they'd support my weight. Once I was steady I rushed over to the others. I was glad to melt into the group so I could think straight.

I was eager to get painting, and soon the process consumed me yet again. I was caught up in the lines and colours, concentrating on the images before me. The mural was beginning to take shape — the different houses were coming to life. We decided to paint the panels in chronological order with the oldest houses on the left, then moving through time to the right. We even thought of a way to use each other's styles. We were going to mix the different styles randomly, creating a collage of contrasts. You'd look at one part and then your eye would see something else that, for a second, didn't belong. But the longer you stared, the less out of place it would seem. At least, that was the goal.

I painted a neighbourhood of row houses and Rachael surrounded each home with trees and a yard. Peter worked on a duplex, trying to add different hues. Throughout the mural, Russell used his lettering to describe each scene while Zach added texture and shading in spots to give depth and change the perspective.

I nodded as I stood back and looked at the work. I had a brainwave: "What if we paint the oldest things in black and white only, then move to sepia, and then to full colour as things get more modern?"

"Yeah, I think that would work," said Peter. He stepped back, beside me, to survey the mural. His freckled hand cupped his freckled chin. "And I'm your guy for the black and white."

"Good idea about the changing colours. But are you sure you're the one for the black and white, Peter?" Russell tilted his head in my direction. "Vic seems to have a thing for black and white, too."

Peter laughed. "Oh, yeah."

"Go for it, Peter. I like to paint with bright colours. This is the only black and white I use." I motioned to my own face.

The three of us laughed.

Maybe this project wasn't such a bad idea, after all.

Again, we had to leave the hoarding and go out to remove "misplaced" art. I headed toward the cruiser with Zach, but Officer Mitchell put out an arm to block me.

"No. Today, you go with Russell and Peter in Cathy's car," he said. I got the feeling he didn't want me hanging out with Zach. *It's none of your business who I hang out with.* Besides, it's not like Zach is any worse than the rest; aren't we here because we're all a bunch of criminals?

I sat in the front with Cathy. Russell and Peter got in the back. The boys chatted easily back and forth, and I listened.

"I got caught again," Peter was telling Russell.

"What?" Russell sounded surprised.

"Yeah. Tagging the side of the grain elevator down by Point Pleasant Park."

"Jeeze, man. Don't blow it now. We've just declared you the best at black and white. We need you for the old stuff."

"I guess the old man's right. I'm destined for jail."

"Forget what he says. Prove him wrong." I looked in the rearview mirror and saw Russell nod at Peter, but Peter didn't look convinced. He slumped in the seat.

Cathy chimed in. "I can put in a good word for you, but only if you promise to keep yourself out of trouble," she said. The guys had been talking as though they'd forgotten she was right there hearing the conversation, too.

"Dunno if I can promise that." Peter slouched even further and gazed out the window. "My Dad drives me nuts. He's never happy with anything I do."

"So, your father gives you a hard time. At least you have one around," Russell said.

I turned and looked directly at Russell. I said those exact words to Zach this morning.

"What do you know?" Peter was angry.

"I know I live in a foster home — my third in four years. My parents can't seem to get it together enough to look after themselves, let alone me." Russell was talking fast, his face flushed. "Dad can't hold a job for more than a few weeks and Mom's an addict. I work hard and get good grades. I'm eighteen in two years and I can get out of foster care, and I'll be damned if I end up on the streets like them."

A hush fell over the car. Then *Don't Worry, Be Happy* started to play. I hastily jabbed at the dial and the silence returned.

Finally, I spoke.

"You guys didn't know each other before this?" I asked.

"Nope," said Russell. Then he sighed and elaborated: "You get good at meeting strangers in foster care. You learn to be nice and see how it goes. It's a survival skill."

He didn't say any more, and neither did Peter. When the car stopped I grabbed the rollers and grey paint from the trunk, thinking graffiti wasn't the only thing we were covering up.

THIRTEEN

When I got home that afternoon there was a strange car in the driveway. I wondered if it was one of the girls Mom went to dinner with last week. I was so busy avoiding her I hadn't even asked how the evening had turned out.

I entered the house and was surprised to see an older woman who looked vaguely familiar standing in the kitchen with Mom. Had I seen her at the hospital? She had grey curly hair and was shorter than me. She was dressed in the standard old-lady-polyester stretch pants and flowered blouse. She and Mom were both trying to talk over each other and Mom didn't look happy. They stopped as soon as they noticed me. The older lady actually jumped at the sight of me.

Now that she was looking directly at me, I recognized her. She was the sweet chocolate-bar-buying lady from Mr. Habib's. Why would she be here talking with Mom?

"Oh my goodness," she breathed. "It's you! The girl from the store!"

"Victoria," Mom cut in, "this is your grandmother, Elsie. She showed up today to tell me you were trying to contact her." Mom glared at me and I knew she'd start yelling once we were alone.

"Excuse me?" I was floored. *No way.* I thought back to all the easygoing conversations I'd had with this lady.

She was kind and friendly, and I always made an effort to speak with her when she came in. Now I find out she is my *grandmother*? I had emailed and asked her *specifically* to call me and not tell Mom. Instead, she waits long enough that I think she isn't going to bother with me at all, and then she shows up, out of the blue, and I find out I already know her. What kind of sick game was I involved in?

"Victoria, say hello to your grandmother." Mom was speaking through gritted teeth. I could tell she was angry. Well, so was I.

"Hey." It was more of a grunt.

"Hello, dear," she said. The surprise was visible in her eyes.

I nodded but didn't speak. I stared at Elsie, trying to make sense of it all.

"I remember you when you were a tiny baby, before Richard left." She smiled. "You were the cutest little thing."

I was fuming. "Whatever."

She probably didn't think I was so cute now. Sure, she was polite at the store, but I bet she was disappointed to find out the girl with the black spiked hair and the face piercings was her own flesh and blood. She was still being polite, but I didn't feel like letting her off the hook so easily.

"And I can tell you think I am still just as cute." My words dripped with sarcasm. How could she stand here and pretend everything was fine? How could she act like we were having a regular conversation at Mr. Habib's? How could she betray me and then show up all sweet and sentimental?

"I'm sure you are confused by all of this," said Elsie carefully. I assumed she was trying for a dear-old-granny smile, but I wasn't buying it.

"You have no idea what I am thinking," I snapped.

"Victoria. Don't be sassy," said Mom. Her eyes were fierce.

"Yes, I suppose that's true," acknowledged Elsie.

I stormed out of the room. I was done with this talk. Out of sight, I leaned against the wall for support. I could hear their conversation.

"Oh dear," fretted Elsie. "Please, Julia, can we just try to get along? There really is no excuse for my letting so much time pass. I did try many times to contact you. I called and sent emails. You always dismissed us, Julia."

"I couldn't bear to see Richard or hear about his life and how he thought he was so much better off without us," answered Mom.

"He may have said that to you at first, but it was never the way it really was. He was miserable and often consumed with guilt for allowing the best thing that ever happened to him slip away." I imagined Elsie reaching over and placing a hand on Mom's shoulder at this point.

"Well *he* never called or tried to reach us." Mom's voice was cracking with emotion.

"You made it clear you didn't want anything to do with him. And he was to keep away from Victoria."

"Because he was still drinking! Once Victoria was on the way we both had to grow up. He didn't." She took a deep breath. "As hard as it was, it was better that way."

My stomach knotted and my throat grew tight. I couldn't stand by and listen any longer. I marched back into the room and the conversation. "Thanks for letting me have a say in the matter, Mom."

"You were a baby."

"And now I am fifteen. Old enough to make my own decisions."

"He doesn't deserve to know you." Mom angrily wiped tears from her eyes and folded her arms across her chest. She turned away from me and looked in the opposite direction.

"Oh, Julia," said Elsie. She stepped closer to Mom. "Please forgive him. He's ill."

This time, I walked out of the room and towards the front door. Mom and Elsie didn't even notice.

I decided right then I wasn't going to wait any longer; I wasn't going to wait for anyone else to make the choice for me. I took out my phone, typed Elsie's name into Canada 411, and found her street address. I stared. It was close.

I headed in the direction of Elsie's house. I walked quickly at first but then I slowed down, my courage wavering. I stopped and scuffed my toe on the sidewalk. I started to turn around, but the thought of Mom and Elsie still at the house stopped me from going back. I rushed on to Elsie's.

When I found the house, I surveyed it from the sidewalk for a moment. It was just a regular bungalow. One I had passed many times before without knowing my "family" lived there. I walked up to the front door and reached out a finger, intending to press the doorbell. But instead I grasped the doorknob. It was unlocked. I entered slowly. It seemed quiet and empty. Then I heard a feeble voice call out, "That you, Mom?"

I jumped. This was a bad idea. *Yeah, well, what was one more bad idea?* I didn't answer the voice, but headed in the direction it came from, down a small hallway. I walked slowly and carefully, staring straight ahead, looking at nothing but the direction I was going.

"Who's there?" said the voice.

It came from the next room. I took a big swallow and wiped my sweaty palms on my pants. I couldn't chicken out now. Not when I was this close.

I peered around the doorway. "It's Vic." The words caught it my throat and were barely audible. I stepped over the threshold and into the room. The walls were white and bare, the furniture sparse — just the bed, a single chair, some medical equipment, and one of those hospital tables that swung over the bed when needed. It was stark and sterile. It was a hospital room in the middle of a home. It felt out of place and awkward in the rest of the house. Like me.

A man was lying in a bed in the centre of the room, his eyes fixed on me. His skin was pale and papery, his cheeks sunken. He looked small and fragile in the bed. He had an oxygen hose around his head and secured in his nostrils. His brown curly hair needed a shampoo and a comb. His lips were cracked and split. I automatically ran my tongue over my own.

I watched his eyes change from fear to recognition as he figured out who I was. He struggled to pull himself into a sitting position.

"Vic…Victoria?" It wasn't more than a whisper.

"Vic." I corrected. I couldn't take my eyes off his. They were sunken and surrounded by dark circles but they were familiar. "Victoria is the queen. I'm not."

"Yeah," he rasped a short laugh. "Your mom and her royal obsession." His voice gathered strength as he talked. "Her folks never really approved of her — or me — so she adopted the royals as her new family. Said they were easier to love. Does she still follow them?"

"She knows more about Harry and William than she does about me."

"Figures. She is a good woman though." He grinned as he spoke of her.

"So good you dumped her and her baby?" My head felt like it might overflow with emotion. My earlier anger was slipping away, quickly being replaced by a deep sadness. I bit my lip, trying to pretend none of this really mattered.

"I was no good for either of you. Still am. It was my mother's idea to get in touch with you."

I turned to leave. "Sorry to bother you then. Guess there's no need of me standing here wondering what to say. You just said it all. So long."

"No. Wait." He shifted in the bed and then winced. He laid back and took a deep breath, slowly letting it out. "That's not what I meant. How can I ask you to come and see me after all this time? It's not fair to you."

"Well, there's something we agree on. But I'm pretty sure we're the only ones. Mom and Elsie are still back at our house arguing."

"Those two always did clash. Guess they're too much alike."

"Oh really? Your mom is never pleased with anything you do, and barely talks to you unless it's to scream? Lucky you."

Richard looked at me closely. He took a breath and said, "I'm sure Julia means well. She's doing the best she can as a single parent. I'm sorry."

"Right. And I'm supposed to believe that." Now I was angry again. "Don't think just because you're sick I'm going to forgive you and fall all over you. I've gotten along all right without you for fifteen years. I can keep going."

"Guess I deserved that."

"Damn right."

"You seem a bit like your old man," he said with a glint in his eye. His smirk made him look mischievous. He had a small dimple on his chin. "Does that tongue get you in trouble?"

"I don't have an old man, thank you very much. And I never knew I had a dad either."

"Well, now you do," he said simply. "So, why all the black? I'm not dead yet."

"You wish this was for you." I waved my hands up and down my body. "This is the way I dress all the time. It's who I am."

"Bullshit. What's with all the makeup? What are you hiding from?"

Oh, I dunno. Mom's disappointment. The unfairness of life. Self-doubt. Pick one, old man.

"Excuse me?" I shot a look at the dying man before me. This question was coming from a man who had been in the same city as his teenage daughter for fifteen years and never bothered to make contact. I don't think so. Who did he think he was?

I whirled around and left. This time I didn't stop. I raced through the house and burst out the front door. I ran down the street wanting to get as far away as I could. I had only known the man for a few minutes and he seemed to know a great deal about me. Well, I wouldn't let him know any more. I was done.

Fourteen

I didn't have the energy to go home and face Mom, but I needed to talk. I thought of Justine, but I knew she was working. I hadn't told Zach about Richard, but maybe it was time I did. He had troubles with his own dad, so surely he'd understand. Just thinking of Zach made me feel better. I texted him to see if he was around to meet up, and he agreed to meet me at Tim's in ten minutes.

I walked in and automatically stood in line. Usually the sweet, sugary smell of donuts and frosting made my stomach growl, but today it made me nauseous. I figured I better eat something, though, so I ordered a sandwich and took a seat. Two men at the table across from me nodded politely, but their eyes were full on condescension. I ignored them.

I picked up the sandwich and brought it to my lips, but I set it back down without taking a bite. I stared at the door, waiting. When I saw Zach, I jumped up and moved toward him. I wrapped my arms around him and squeezed. He hugged me back, triggering the release of all the emotions I had been holding back. I cried. Not a soft weeping, but a real ugly cry: sobbing loud enough to draw attention.

"Hey. It's okay." Zach's voice was warm and comforting on my ear. He rubbed my back and murmured, "Whatever it is, it's okay."

I relaxed against him. When I finally caught my breath and pulled back, people were staring. I was sure my makeup was more frightful than ever; mascara running down my white cheeks. I swiped at my nose and ran a finger under my eyes. The two men at the table across from where I'd been sitting whispered to each other, but loud enough to hear.

"Kids today. Terrible."

"Probably drugs or some other trouble."

I didn't say anything, but Zach was not so tolerant. "Really?" he barked at the men. "What do you know about her? What gives you the right to judge us?"

I tugged on his arm. I didn't want to make a scene, but if felt glorious to have him defend me and use the word "us."

But Zach was on a roll. He spoke loudly so other patrons could hear. I figured he was trying to embarrass the men. "Perhaps you are two dirty old men hanging out at Tim's on a Saturday night hoping to hit on an innocent girl."

One of the men stood up. "Now listen here, young man —"

"No. You listen," Zach cut across him. "Keep your opinions to yourself and mind your own business." He took my hand and we stalked out. We got in his car and he peeled away from the parking lot.

"Thanks," I said reaching for his hand. "But you really didn't have to do that. I get that stuff all the time. Looking different sets you up for ridicule." I flipped down the visor, looking in the mirror to check what was left of my makeup.

"Doesn't make it right." Zach was still annoyed so I stayed quiet for a minute. He drove to a nearby park and we got out. We walked for a bit, step in step, hand in hand, and then sat on the side of a grassy hill.

Zach put an arm around my shoulders and pulled me close. "So, what's up?"

It spilled out of me. I told him everything about Mom, James, Richard, and Elsie. By the time I was done the blue sky was streaked with yellow, orange, and pink. Zach never questioned any of it, he just listened. I was glad I had met him when I did and that I had him to talk to. I thought of the others in the group.

"Did you know Russell lived in a foster home?" I asked.

"Yeah. He mentioned it." Zach leaned back then laid down and stared up at the stars that were starting to blossom in the sky.

"Do you think anyone has a normal family instead of all this crap?" I laid back beside him.

Zach rolled over to face me, his bent arm propping up his head so he looked directly at me. "I think crap *is* normal when it comes to families."

"Maybe." I was still looking straight up; the sky was alive with twinkling stars. "Pretty, isn't it?"

"Yes, it is." Zach kept looking at me. Then he leaned down and kissed me.

We continued to talk and make out and watch the sky. I could have stayed forever, but when I started to yawn Zach insisted he take me home.

He parked in front of my place and we sat there quietly for a minute. Then he squeezed my hand and just said: "Vic, it'll all work out."

"I don't know." I wanted to believe him.

I kissed him lightly and got out of the car. The house was quiet when I let myself in. I wasn't sure if Mom was home and asleep or out. I was too tired to care. I washed my face and crawled into bed. It had been a long day.

I woke up Sunday feeling like I hadn't slept a wink. Thoughts of my dying father weighed heavy on my mind, but thoughts of Zach defending me, comforting me, kissing me, made me float through the house to the kitchen. Mom was at the table. There was no avoiding her.

"Hey," I said warily.

"Did you go see your father yesterday?" she demanded. She set down her teacup and sat up straight in the chair, ready for a confrontation.

Good morning to you too. "Yeah." I spoke calmly. I didn't have it in me to argue.

"I wish you would have discussed it with me first."

"You were busy fighting with his mother," I reminded her. "Whatever, it doesn't matter. I'm not going back to see him again."

"Why not?" Mom seemed to sizzle with anger. "Did Richard say something?"

"I shouldn't have gone in the first place. And Elsie, or Grandmother, or whoever she is, shouldn't have told you I emailed her." I got a glass from the cupboard and poured myself some orange juice.

"She was just trying to do the right thing, Victoria," Mom reasoned. "She didn't want you going behind my back."

I looked at Mom but didn't answer.

"Elsie feels there have been enough secrets." Mom was standing now.

I nodded. "Well, now we all know. You lied to me about Richard and I tried to go behind your back. Guess we're even." I took my juice and went back to my room.

Fifteen

On Monday Mr. Fawthrope handed back our English tests. I stared at the big red *F*. I'd never failed a test before. It was like swallowing a mixture of glass and rocks. It stung and tore at my insides and was heavy in my gut. I had always tried to do my best at school. It was my ticket out of here, my hope for the future, and now I might have jeopardized it.

"Please see me after class, Victoria," said Mr. Fawthrope.

"Can't," I lied. "Busy." There was no way I was going to discuss my tragic life with Mr. Fawthope.

I set the paper on my desk and reached into my backpack for my book.

Kate noticed the grade. "Wow, the mighty Vic has fallen. Maybe hanging out with a bunch of delinquents is rubbing off on you."

"Oh, shut up," I snapped. "You don't know any of those people."

Mark turned around. "I think it's time to ease up on the eye makeup, Vic. Obviously it has sunk in and turned even your grey matter to black."

"You guys are *so* funny."

Jeremy leaned over. "Thanks for noticing. We're here Monday through Friday." He nodded at Mark. The two of them chuckled.

Mr. Fawthrope began to introduce the next book we'd be reading, *Lord of the Flies* by William Golding.

"This is a story of a group of young boys who get stranded on an island and set up their own society."

Maybe I could get stranded on an island...it would be quiet and drama-free. I picked up my pencil and began to doodle. My island had palm trees and sandy beaches, gentle waves, and lots of sun. I kept sketching, filling in detail, daydreaming about the blissful solitude.

The sudden scraping sound of chair startled me. *Focus, Goth Girl, you don't want to fail another test.*

"You see," Mr. Fawthrope continued, "life often hands out unexpected blows. It's how you choose to deal with them that makes all the difference."

Easy to say when you're not the one getting pummelled.

Mr. Fawthrope handed copies of the book out and we had the rest of the period to read silently. When the bell rang, I rushed from the classroom. I plunked my tray down on the table across from Justine. I nodded at her and she gestured in return, but she didn't take out her ear buds.

I watched Justine close her eyes and move her head to what I assumed was the rhythm of the "great new song" she was listening to. Finally, she stopped and took out the earphones.

"Hey," I said.

"Did you know there's going to be a metal festival in Halifax this summer?" Justine blew on the bowl of soup in front of her. She picked up the little square package of crackers, squashed it, then opened it and dumped the crumbs into the bowl.

"No, can't say that I did."

"Yeah! I'm saving up for tickets." She stirred as she spoke.

"Woo-hoo," I said with a laugh. "Extra shifts at Walmart!"

Justine laughed too. "Be glad I work there, or you'd have no paint supplier." She slurped her soup.

"I am. That reminds me, I forgot to mention there were three young guys in the store the other day asking about getting some paint."

Justine stopped eating and looked directly into my eyes. "You didn't say anything did you? I could lose my job."

"I told them to get lost. I'd never rat you out. I need all the people on my side I can muster."

Justine sighed with relief. She stared, waiting for me to elaborate.

"What?" But I knew what she wanted hear. Where should I begin? It seemed like a lifetime of events had happened since I last saw Justine.

"You know what." Justine leaned forward. "Tell me!"

Funny how all this stuff in my life had got the two of us talking. We were almost like friends now. I hadn't expected that. I took a deep breath and sat back.

Justine looked at me expectantly, anxious for me to start.

"Okay, okay. The highlights: Saturday morning, Zach picked me up at home — amazing. Art group — good. After group I came home to find my grandmother there talking to Mom about the card, my email, and me meeting my dad. I left and went to meet my 'dad' — bad idea. I messaged Zach and we spent the evening under the stars talking and making out — best night ever." I made jazz hands.

Justine's eyes were huge and her jaw hung open. I spent the rest of the lunch period filling in the details and answering her questions.

I had to work Wednesday evening. I was trying hard to focus. I really needed this job. Mr. Habib was still at the store doing some paperwork, but I think he stayed late to keep an eye on me.

I kept busy, cleaning when there were no customers. I wiped down the pop cooler and swept the floor. I was replenishing the candy shelves and I headed out back to the stockroom for more chocolate bars. I heard the door chime. I grabbed the box and headed back to the front of the store. Just as I came around the corner I saw the person who had entered.

I froze. It was Elsie. Thankfully she was looking the other way and didn't see me. It was so weird that I had had several conversations with her, not knowing she was my grandmother. Now that I knew, I didn't want to speak with her. I retreated into the stockroom and pretended I hadn't heard anything. I held my breath until I heard Mr. Habib speak to her. He was probably ticked that I hadn't run out like I was supposed to, but I couldn't face her.

I peeked around the corner to see what was happening. Elsie was looking around the store. She rarely bought anything except for the chocolate bars so I figured she was looking for me. Did she know all along that I worked here and just kept coming just to check up on me? Anger started to rise in my throat, but I managed to squash it. No, she had been genuinely surprised the other day. She didn't know the girl at the store dressed in black and covered with scary makeup was her long-lost granddaughter.

Mr. Habib rang her through, handed her a bag, and wished her a nice evening. Elsie took her purchase and left.

When I finally came out, Mr. Habib looked at me closely. "Didn't you hear the door?"

"Oh. No. Sorry." I clumsily unpacked the box of bars I had brought out from the stockroom and began cramming them on the rack.

Mr. Habib grumbled and went back to his paperwork.

Sixteen

It was week five of the project already. Zach texted me to say he'd meet me there. He'd had an argument with his father, and his dad wouldn't let him take the car.

As I got ready, I stared at Goth Girl in the mirror. I liked her blue eyes and how they stood out against the white foundation and crimson lipstick. I liked doing things differently than the majority of kids in school, and I sure couldn't help what others thought of the look. It felt good to think that Zach liked me. Just the thought of him made my heart beat faster and my palms sweat.

Russell and Peter were standing by the half-painted fence when I got there.

"Hey, look, it's Dumb and Dumber." I teased good-naturedly. After hearing the two of them talk in Cathy's car last week, I had reconsidered my first impressions.

"Nice, coming from Dracula's niece," was Peter's clap-back.

"Clever! You're smarter than you look." I turned to Russell. "I bet you are too."

"I'll never tell." Russell grinned.

"Well, we know we're all great artists. Look at this fence." I made a gesture with my hand like I was showing off a new car, pretending to be a model.

"Sorry, Vic," Russell snickered, "I don't think you are model material."

"I'm crushed." I said with mock sadness. I brought my hand to my brow and feigned a cry.

"Speaking of models, here comes Rachael," said Peter as he watched her prance towards us.

"What's everyone talking about?" she asked.

"Just admiring the view." Peter whistled and nodded. "And I like what I see."

"Well, you can look, but you can't touch." Rachael tossed her hair. "You're not what I'm looking for."

"Hey, what's that supposed to mean?" Peter stood up straight and puffed out his chest.

"Ratty jeans and a juvenile T-shirt?" Rachael wrinkled her nose. "I don't think so."

"Nothing wrong with jeans and a T-shirt," said Russell looking down at his own attire.

Rachael didn't say a word, but the disgusted look on her face made the hair on the back of my neck stand up. I'd seen that same look on my mother's face, when she was looking at me. Maybe I wasn't good at speaking up for myself with my mother, but I sure wasn't going to stand by while Rachael judged these guys.

"Hey. You'd be lucky to date one of these guys. Maybe there's more to them than you think." *Just like all of us.*

"Wow, Vic. I didn't know you felt that way." Russell moved closer and put his hand on my shoulder and gave me an exaggerated look of smouldering eyes.

"Too late." I turned to see Zach arriving. "She's taken." He gave me a kiss.

Russell backed off, throwing his hands in the air. Rachael eyed Zach and pouted.

Cathy arrived with our painting supplies, and everyone fell

silent as we got to work. The only talk was of which colour to use where and what details to add to each scene.

When we took a break, I walked over to Zach. He had just finished a section on the modern end of the mural. I reached up and wiped a spot of paint from his cheek.

"Look, there's white paint on your face. I knew it wouldn't be long before you wanted to look like me." I winked.

"That's what happens. Couples start to look like one another." He wrapped one arm around me. My stomach did a backflip to hear him call us a couple. I could get used to this.

Officer Mitchell cleared his throat. "We are just here to paint, folks," he reminded us. "Save the romance for your own time."

"Prude," whispered Zach.

The cop gave him a look and kept moving.

I gave Zach a quick kiss. It would take more than Officer Mitchell to keep me away from my boyfriend.

SEVENTEEN

"Victoria Markham," hollered Mom on Sunday morning, waking me.

Oh no. It couldn't be good if Mom was using my full name. I crawled out of bed and made my way to the kitchen. She probably wanted to rehash the subject of "Dad." *Good luck with that.*

"Yeah?" I wiped the sleep from my eyes and headed toward the fridge.

"What do you have to say for yourself?" Mom stood glaring at me, with one hand on her hip.

I shrugged. I could tell she was pissed, but I had no idea why. "I'm hungry?"

"Don't be sassy. Officer Mitchell called to say he was glad you made it to the community art project yesterday and that things seemed to be going well." She paused, holding back her bombshell. "Then he mentioned a couple of weeks ago you tried to take off. He mentioned a boy being a bad influence."

"I was just going to get something to eat with a friend. No big deal." I opened the fridge, peered inside, and closed the door, not finding anything. I reached for the cupboard to grab a granola bar, but changed my mind. I'd suddenly lost my appetite. *Here we go again with a one-sided conversation.* And what was up with Officer Mitchell? I wish he'd mind his own damn business.

"It *is* a big deal." Mom got louder. "You know you have to do this art thing. I thought you liked to paint." Mom's voice was dripping with sarcasm.

Now it was my turn to raise my voice. "I *do* like to paint. It's just that I thought some of the other kids were lame and I wanted to go to the mall. In the end, I didn't miss anything, so forget it." I started to walk away. There was no sense in even trying to make her understand.

"Victoria, I meant what I said before: after this, the painting's done. I don't need you spending your time 'creating art' instead of doing what's important. Do you hear me?"

"Yes. I hear you, Mom. Loud and clear."

"And we aren't done talking about your father, either. Elsie called again. He's asking about you."

Yeah, but he didn't call. I stomped up the stairs back to my room. *You think you can tell me not to paint, Mom? No way.* I slammed my bedroom door and grabbed my sketchpad. Why do I have to do whatever pleases her instead of me? And why do I have to go and see a father I thought was dead just because he might be dying?

Eventually, I had to get dressed and go to work. It was great to have an excuse to leave the house. As I walked the couple of blocks to the store, I kept thinking of Zach. I read and re-read the texts we'd been sending.

"Morning." I sent a new text, not even sure if he'd be up yet.

His reply was almost instant. "Hey. Off to work?"

"Yeah."

"Miss you." He even included a smiley face.

I looked around. If anyone saw me they would wonder why I was grinning like a maniac at my phone.

I worked my shift and then headed straight to Walmart. I'd already filled my sketchbook and needed a new one.

I grabbed the book and walked back through the clothing section. I could use a new shirt — black of course. As I passed the dresses, I thought of the security guard from my last visit. I wondered if the jerk was working today.

A familiar voice made me turn around. I couldn't believe my eyes. There was Rachael, talking with an older version of herself. There they were with their long hair perfectly combed, their eyelashes fluttering. The older one was dressed in a stunning outfit. Way overdressed for Walmart. I hid behind a rack of chunky knit sweaters.

"Here, try this," said the lady. "The pattern is gorgeous." She thrust a dress at Rachael.

"I don't know, Mom." Rachael put her hand out to take the garment. "It's kind of skimpy."

"It's not skimpy, it's flattering. As I always say: if you've got it, flaunt it and, you've got it, my darling." Rachael's mom swept over to another rack, the hangers clacking as she sorted through more dresses. "We're having the Johnsons over for dinner next week, and they're bringing their son. This dress will get you noticed, and he's such a nice young man." She stopped moving hangers and fixed her daughter with a meaningful look. "He's going to study medicine."

"I don't need a nice young man."

"Of course you do, darling. You're too young to understand, but every girl needs a man to look after her. Why do you think we spend so much time and energy to look pretty?"

"I can look after myself."

"Nonsense. Go." She placed her hand on Rachael's back and moved her toward the fitting room. "Just try it on." Rachael looked exhausted. It was the kind of look only a mother could evoke.

I had never considered Rachael didn't want to look like a walking Barbie doll. She was so good at it I figured it was genuine.

I called Zach. "I just saw Rachael and her mom buying a new dress."

"Big deal." He sounded uninterested.

"I think she puts on the bimbo show to please her mother."

"Probably. So?"

"It just kind of made me think about how little I really know people." I hated people judging me and yet I was doing the same thing. It was nice to know I had someone to call and chat with about stuff like this. "She's a great artist. I wonder how she ended up at group. She doesn't strike me as someone who'd have the guts to break the law."

"I have no idea." Zach's tone was flat. He clearly didn't want to spend his time talking about Rachael, so I dropped the subject. We talked about the mural as I walked home. When I finally said goodbye and hung up, my smile faded. I missed him already.

That evening, I sat on the edge of my bed, waiting for Mom to go to sleep. I looked around and realized things in my room hadn't changed much in the last few years, even though I had. I still had the soft pink comforter and the big fluffy pillows. But two things were different: a huge graffiti poster hung on the ceiling above my bed, and one of James's paintings was on the wall beside my desk. After rescuing it from the pile on the living room floor the day he left, I had repaired the torn canvas and glued the frame back together. I had kept the painting safely stored in my closet until this morning. After Mom yelled at me this time, I took it out and hung it on the wall across from my bed so I could easily see it as a reminder that I was a painter, like

James. He was more of a father to me than Richard had ever been. He was there when I needed him. Or last least, he used to be.

I waited and listened. Mom's nightly routine rarely changed: iron a uniform, shower, dry her hair, brew a cup of tea, read for a bit, then lights out. Today it seemed to take longer than usual, because I was eager to leave. The mural painting was great, but I hadn't done graffiti since the night I met Officer Mitchell. I wanted to smell the aerosol and see if I could feel the excitement of doing what I shouldn't.

I texted Zach and he agreed to meet me. I grabbed my spray paint from its hiding place in the bottom drawer of my dresser and stuffed the cannons in my backpack. I slipped out the door and headed toward the overpass.

When I got there I took a deep breath, smelling the salty harbour as I shook the can. I tried to think of something to paint, but nothing came to mind. The rush of excitement didn't come either. I placed my hand on the rough surface of the concrete. It was cold, hard, and lifeless like the grey that now covered it. I stood there and closed my eyes, imagining the artwork underneath and the passion I'd felt the night I put it there. I turned my back to the wall and sat, bringing my knees to my chest and hugging them tightly. The thrill of illegal graffiti was gone. I didn't want to pour my heart into something only to see it wiped out in a few days. I didn't want to be just another "rebellious teen." And besides, I was too distracted: breaking the law wasn't going to help me figure out what to do about Richard.

I waited for Zach, shivering in the damp fog. The light of my cell startled me out of my reverie, but I was relieved to read the words, "be right there."

Instead of Zach's car, I saw a familiar shiny SUV slow down with the blinker flashing. *Shit.* Zach's father must have caught him sneaking out and now he was coming to give me a piece of his mind. I held my breath as the SUV pulled over and crunched to a stop on the gravel. I stood up, but didn't move toward the vehicle, watching the driver's window lower.

"Hey, you look like you just saw a ghost." Zach smiled and his eyes sparkled.

That look made me tingle, and I had to focus to keep my feet on the ground. Relief poured through me. I raced toward the car, opened the passenger door, jumped in, and threw my arms around Zach. "I'm so glad to see you. I thought it was your dad and you were in trouble again."

"What? Me in trouble? Never." He laughed nervously.

I sighed. Yes, this is just what I needed. I squeezed his hand and kissed him. His lips were warm and I forgot the damp chill of the evening.

"I'm glad you texted me," said Zach, kissing me back.

"Me too."

He drove to Tim Horton's and parked the car. We didn't go in, but walked back to the overpass. Zach took one of the cans of paint. He quickly sprayed "Vic + Zach" and drew a heart around it. It was sloppy and the paint dripped. I loved it in theory, but wished he had taken his time. It reminded me of the scribbles the group had covered up the other day. It wasn't art.

"Aren't you going to paint?" asked Zach.

I shrugged. "Don't really feel like it right now. Let's just grab a coffee instead."

We walked back to the SUV and ordered coffee in the drive-thru. We drove to a nearby park —*our park*— but we stayed in the car.

Zach was the first to speak. "So what's up?"

I launched into it. "Mom and I had a fight. She doesn't want me to paint at all. So I went out to do graffiti…but I couldn't do it. It didn't feel right. I want to paint, but I don't want to see it wasted again. I am so confused. Plus, I miss James and I want a father. But how could my real dad stay away for my whole life?"

The words came out fast, and it felt good to share.

"Wow. My bad girl is losing her touch," Zach said. He held my hand, bringing it to his lips and kissing the back of it. Each spot he kissed felt hot, even after he stopped. "Yeah, I guess." I snuggled closer and closed my eyes.

Zach didn't offer any solutions. There weren't any easy answers. We sat in comfortable silence for a few minutes. Then he said, "Hey, guess what I did?"

"What?"

He reached into the back seat, grabbed his notebook, and handed it to me. "I did that sketch of you."

I opened the book and couldn't believe the beautiful young woman looking back at me. Her short hair fell around her face and her eyes looked bright and alive. One side of her mouth was raised slightly in a mischievous half-smile that made you wonder what was on her mind.

"That's me. You did all this from memory?" I asked, awestruck. "It's incredible."

"When you have a gorgeous subject to work with, it's easy. I don't want to forget what you looked like that morning."

"Do I really look like that?" It had been a long time since I really looked at myself without goth makeup. Putting it on was as routine as getting out of bed in the morning.

"Yes, you do." Zach pulled me close, put his hand on my chin, and gently tilted my face up. He looked into my eyes for a moment before kissing me deeply. The windows began to fog up with our breathing.

Suddenly, a loud rap on the window and a bright light interrupted us.

We both jumped.

"What the...." Zach turned the key in the ignition and pushed the button to lower the window.

Standing by the window was Officer Mitchell.

"Hello, Officer Mitchell," said Zach politely. "Nice to see you out on this lovely evening."

"Cut the bull, Zach. You know why I'm here." He was all business. He aimed the beam of his flashlight at me. "Victoria, did you know this car was stolen?"

"Stolen? No way, it belongs to Zach's dad." My mouth went dry and I felt my heart pound in my ears. The chill was back and I shivered.

"That's the thing. It belongs to Zach's dad, not Zach. He did not have permission to take it this evening." He looked back at Zach. "This is a serious crime."

"I can't believe he called the cops." Zach laughed bitterly.

"Well, he did. So now we have to take you to the station," said Officer Mitchell.

"But —" I was trembling. I couldn't process what was happening.

"And *you* are going home." The cop looked at me like I was a misbehaving child. "My partner will give you a lift."

Zach got out and climbed into the back seat of the cruiser. Officer Mitchell's partner got in the driver's seat of the SUV and buckled his seatbelt. I clung to Zach's sketchpad. I wanted to do or say something tough — defend Zach or tell the cops to screw off. But I knew it was useless. The black eye makeup and spiked hair failed me.

Eighteen

I couldn't believe Zach's dad had him arrested. I sent Zach a couple of texts but got no reply. I bet his dad had taken away his phone too. My thoughts drifted to my own father and the image of him sick in bed. I toyed with the idea of going back to Elsie's house. My head was saying *no way — he abandoned me and I don't owe him anything.* But then my heart would bleed, thinking Richard's time might be short and I'd convince myself I would regret it forever if I didn't go.

In history class on Tuesday, Mr. Jones talked about Pier 21 and family trees again. I doodled on my notebook. *My family tree is a cactus, full of thorns.* Again, my thoughts drifted back to my father.

"That's my seat."

I looked up, startled. Some guy was talking to me. "What?"

"The bell rang five minutes ago. Don't tell me you're so excited about history, you're gonna sit through another class?"

Wow. I missed the bell and all the people leaving? I needed to figure out this stuff about Richard before it wrecked my whole academic year.

"Just keeping the seat warm for you." I got up and gave the

guy a lame smile as I headed for the hallway. I had to jog to get to my next class in time.

At lunch, Justine seemed quiet. "What's up?" I asked.

She shook her head and rolled her eyes. She didn't take out her ear buds.

I picked at my fries. The more I looked at her, the more I thought about it. Justine had spent most every lunch hour for the last few weeks listening to me; it was time to return the favour.

"Did you buy your tickets for that festival yet?" I leaned forward and spoke a bit louder so she'd hear me over the music.

She nodded.

"What do you wear to a concert like that?"

Justine put both arms out and motioned with her hands to say, "This is it." But she still didn't speak or take out the earphones.

"Did you find someone to go with?" I was determined to get her to talk.

"There's a girl at work who likes metal too." She looked down at her food like she wanted to ignore me.

Hmmm, this is tough. I reached forward and touched her arm so she'd have to look at me. "So, do you stick with fuchsia for the concert? Or go with another colour? Maybe black like me." I pointed to my own spiked hair.

Finally, Justine took out one earpiece. "Maybe another colour, but not black. That's all you." She cracked a smile. "Thanks for prying. I just finished a math test and I'm not sure if I passed." She paused, and then said, "I need the credit to graduate. I really don't want to have to take it again next year."

I nodded. "Well, you really seemed to be getting the hang of it when we were going over it last week. Just wait and see, you never know!"

"Yeah. Miracles can happen, right?" Justine smirked again

and we chatted until the bell rang, but I opted to keep my continuing saga to myself this time.

When I got home I rechecked my phone for anything from Zach. Nothing. Maybe he didn't have his phone, but he could have sent me an email. I went to the computer and checked. Nothing.

"Man, this sucks," I said to no one. I needed to get out and walk. I couldn't wait around for someone else to make the next move. It was up to me, and I knew what I needed to do.

I grabbed my jacket and left the house. I shivered and rubbed my arms; it was damp and cold. *Whoever said spring in Halifax is lovely clearly wasn't from here.* I walked quickly down the street, allowing my feet to take me where I needed to go.

I knocked, but no one answered. I tried the doorknob. It was unlocked, so I took that as an unspoken invitation and entered the little house. This time I looked around, taking in the decor. The contrast between this place and home was pretty stark: here, the couch was big and soft-looking. A homemade afghan lay across the back. Living plants sprouted happily from brightly coloured pots, and the walls were covered with art — real paintings, not just lame reproductions of the royal family. It looked welcoming and comfortable instead of creepy and stiff.

I studied the artwork. Some were oils, some were acrylics, and there was even a watercolour. They were good. I squinted at the bottom corner of each piece and noticed they were all signed with the same initials — R. M.

I stared. My mind raced. Then it hit me like a brick wall: Richard Markham. My father was a painter too. No wonder Mom has such a thing against me painting. She had developed a bad track record with artists. I continued down the hallway angry at the lies, hurt by the omissions, and startled by the realization that I had so much in common with this so-called "father" of mine.

I walked towards the room I knew was Richard's, noticing more paintings lining the walls. These ones featured people: a little blonde girl on a swing set at the park, the same little girl running in a meadow with an older lady, maybe her mother, chasing butterflies. I stopped. I gasped as I looked down the length of the hall. There must have been ten paintings, all depicting the same blonde girl. She was shown at different ages and in different scenes, but they were all the same person. I was certain.

I was certain because they were all me.

I stormed into Richard's room. He was in bed, propped up on pillows against the frame. There were more paintings in here, and there was even an easel set up with a new painting in progress. This one didn't show the little blonde girl, but a half-finished teenage girl, clad in all black, wearing heavy, dark eye makeup.

I didn't even say hello. "Who is the little blonde girl in all the pictures?" I demanded, facing him full on. I wanted to see his face when he answered.

"How should I know?" He snapped back.

"Your initials are on all the paintings." I pointed to the pictures in the room. "Who. Is. The. Girl. In. All. Of. The. Paintings?" I knew and he knew, but I wanted to hear him say it.

"It's you, okay?" His voice was defiant. Then it softened. "It's you. Your mother always liked the park. We went when we were together, so I imagined she still took you there when you were a little girl."

"Did you *stalk* us? That is creepy." My voice was louder than I wanted. I hated admitting that this bothered me. My throat grew tight, cutting off my speech. My stomach knotted. He had all these images of me and my life, but I had none of him.

"No, I didn't stalk you," he said. "Your mother sent photos once or twice in the beginning. I imagined you being happy and carefree, swinging and running all day. I painted pictures to pretend it was true." He paused. "And to pretend I could be a part of it."

I took a deep breath and found my voice. "Wow. You and Mom are a fine pair. You both spend so much time caught up in your imaginations that you miss the reality. She thinks the royals are her family, and you think yours is in a tube of paint."

"Maybe. So what is the reality? You seem awfully interested in *my* artwork. Do you like to paint?"

I hesitated. I couldn't trust him, and if I let him know details about me it would only set me up to be hurt even more. All my life I had been wondering what it would be like to have a father. Now here he was, but I wasn't sure I wanted him in my life. I continued looking at him. His arms were thin and his shirt bagged with extra material. He had moved to sit on the side of the bed, and he had taken the oxygen tubes out of his nostrils.

"Can you go without that?" I asked, nodding at the tank and tangle of tubes.

"For a while. I've been having a few good days. I've even taken up painting again." He motioned toward the easel.

I turned toward the picture and studied it, this time, as an artist. He'd done a great job with colour, considering his palate was limited by the subject. He had managed to capture the eyes. They looked real, had a glint of mischief even. He had nailed the spiky hair and the piercings were perfectly placed. And the smile had that crooked tilt. I was impressed he could infer what my grin looked like, considering I hadn't been here that long for my first visit. And I sure hadn't smiled.

I was flattered. The knot in my stomach loosened a bit. I considered answering his question. I recalled our last conversation. He had admitted he was at fault and this whole thing was not fair. That was more than Mom ever did. Maybe I would just stay for a minute. I could always turn and run away. It's not like he could chase after me.

"Yeah, I paint."

He smiled and nodded like he already knew.

"I got picked up by the cops for my work in fact."

"Graffiti?"

"Yeah, under the overpass by the MacKay."

"No kidding? That's ballsy."

"Not really." I began to relax slightly. "I got caught and now I'm in this community art program. A bunch of us are doing a mural around a construction site and we have to spend time removing graffiti."

"So, are you any good?"

"What do you think?" It's too hard for an artist to answer that question, especially when another artist is asking.

"I think you're probably a great artist. And it surprises the hell out of you." He paused and took a sip of water from a plastic cup on the bedside table. "You wonder how something so beautiful came from you."

"You seem to be pretty sure of that." I took a seat in the chair next to the bed. My shoulders released the tension they had been holding. For a man who just met me, he sure seemed to know me.

"Because it's exactly how I feel: these pictures are beautiful because they are of you and I created them. And I helped create *you*. I sure made my share of mistakes, but you are not one of them."

I didn't respond. I didn't know how to reply to that.

"I wish things could have been different," he said, pleading. "But I can't change the past. And now, my future is short. But you have a lifetime. If you love to paint, then paint. But make the painting count." He leaned forward a bit. "And most of all, stop hiding, Vic. Don't be afraid to let people know who you really are."

"Is that why you had Elsie contact me? Because *you* wanted to stop hiding?"

"Yes. I know it's too late, but I wanted you to know who I was."

I swallowed hard and blinked back tears. I did want to know him. More than anything. But now he might die. I wasn't sure if I could handle that on top of everything else.

"Well, now I know. So, I guess that's all." I got up and turned to leave. "I gotta go."

I walked slowly, hoping he'd stop me and beg me to stay. He did not. I walked down the hallway toward the front door.

As soon as the door closed behind me, I began to run. I ran and ran, trying to get ahead of the ache in my heart. But no matter how fast I went, I seemed a step behind.

By the time I reached my house my lungs were burning but I was certain of two things: I would go back to see my father again, and it would hurt like hell when he died. All I could do was focus on the space between.

Nineteen

The rest of the week passed in a blur. I thought of Dad and all the things I wanted to know about him. I thought of Zach and wondered what had happened since he'd gotten picked up by the police.

I couldn't wait to see Zach. Even though his dad was crazy enough to have his own son arrested, I still hoped he'd let Zach come to the art project. It was one thing to ground him or take away his phone, but surely he'd want Zach to finish his community service hours. Zach had actually started taking part in the painting, even though he told us all he didn't really care. And his painting was good. He worked well with Rachael's realistic style and the cartoons I'd created. He was great at standing back and showing the rest of us where to fill in empty spots or lighten up dark areas.

I arrived at the mural a little early, and Zach was already there. I rushed over and threw my arms around his neck, breathing a sigh of relief that I had been holding for days.

"Sorry about the other night." Zach gave me a quick peck on the cheek, but he didn't put his arms around me. He seemed distracted. "Dad and I had just had one of our usual fights that night and he took my car keys. So I grabbed his keys and took the SUV." He looked at me and gave me a small smile. "I really wanted to see you and I'm tired of my father thinking he's the boss."

"What's gonna happen?"

"I'm grounded with no keys or phone. Dad says he's going to stick with the theft charges, but I think he's bluffing. He'll let me stew for a while, and then he'll call his lawyer and have the whole thing looked after." Zach tried to sound convincing, but the cocky edge was missing.

"And what if he doesn't call if off? Do you know what'll happen?"

"At worst, I'll go to juvie."

I repressed a shudder and squeezed him a little tighter. I didn't bother to ask why he hadn't tried to contact me.

"It's nothing. I hear it's a great place." He put one arm around me. "The food's good and they have a gym. I can use the time to work out. It seems I have been thinking of other things lately and my muscles are getting soft." He looked at me and winked. "Don't worry about a thing." Zach shifted from one foot to the other as he looked off in the distance.

"What about your sister, if you go away?" I squeezed his hand. There seemed to be more that Zach wasn't saying, but I had no idea what it might be.

"I'll think of something." Zach smiled, but it didn't reach his eyes.

He seemed deflated. I decided to change the subject. "I went to see my father again."

"How'd it go?" Zach searched my eyes for the answer before I could speak, and it made me relax. This was the Zach I knew from the night under the stars. The gentle, concerned guy I fell for.

"He's a painter!"

Zach stepped back. "What! Really?"

I nodded. "And a good one, too. He has all of these painting of me that he's done over the years. Apparently, he painted them from pictures Mom sent him."

"Smart man, using a great subject." Zach stood taller and puffed out his chest. "We *artistes* know a good subject when we see one." He smiled and I noticed it reached his eyes this time.

"He's working on one now of me in goth."

"Well, I guess I'll have to get busy and do one too." The return of Zach's cocky grin made me melt. I hoped that whatever was bothering him a few minutes ago was forgotten.

As we laughed the others arrived and we got to work on the mural. It got quiet as our attention was absorbed by the art in front of us. My only thoughts were of colour choice, shading, and contrast. But my concentration was broken when Russell spoke.

"What do you think of this?" Russell asked Zach, pointing to the spot on the fence he was painting. Russell was trying some cartooning which wasn't his usual style, and we'd all gotten used to bouncing ideas off of Zach.

"I think this is all a waste of time," Zach replied bitterly. "And you should stop asking me dumb questions." I guess he hadn't forgotten what was bugging him.

"Hey, take it easy, man." Peter walked over toward Zach and Russell. "No need to get your pricey knickers in a knot."

"Shut up, punk." Zach stormed toward Peter with his fists clenched.

Peter stood his ground. "Go ahead, hit me. See if it makes you feel better." Peter taunted Zach by moving his chin forward. I held my breath, afraid of what might happen next.

"Knock it off, guys." Russell moved between the two of them. "Forget it. Just paint." He placed his hands on Zach's chest, trying to move him back a bit.

"I'm just tired of this whole thing," Zach said as he stepped back.

"Well, we're almost done. Don't quit on us now, man," urged Russell.

"Fine." Zach's shoulders relaxed slightly. He picked up a brush, but instead of the fence he pretended to paint Peter. Russell hooted when Peter ducked and all three bumped fists and went back to work.

I released the breath I had been holding and stepped back to take in the whole mural. Our individual talents were good, but the combined effect was awesome. This was more than just a painting — it was part of us for others to see. I liked that. My chest swelled with pride. I might even miss these guys when it was all over.

I worked along the mural and moved closer to Rachael. I admired the Navy ship and dock she was working on. "Nice job," I said sincerely, nodding toward the picture.

Rachael gave me her sweet smile and tossed her hair back. "Thanks," she cooed.

"Ugh, stop," I said to her. "Just be yourself. There's no one to impress." I didn't want to say that I had seen her with her mom the other day, but I wanted to somehow let her know I knew it was all an act and that it wasn't necessary. At least, it wasn't necessary with me. "We're just two girls painting a fence. That's enough."

"Whatever." She returned to the work.

I watched as she seemed to focus on the art. She added a Canadian flag that looked like it was blowing in the wind to the vessel. "I hear Zach's in a heap of trouble with his dad." She looked over at the three boys.

"How'd you hear that?" *Man, news sure travels fast.*

"Oh, I talked to Zach on Monday. He had to spend the night at the police station because his dad wouldn't even go get him." She glanced at me from under her eyelashes. "He was pretty upset."

I couldn't believe my ears. I had tried and tried to reach Zach with no luck. How'd she manage to talk to him? I put my hand on her brush and she turned to look at me. "How'd you get to talk to Zach? His dad took away his phone and he was grounded."

Rachael laughed her tinkling princess laugh. The show was back on. "I'm Zach's neighbour. I've lived beside his family for years. I'm only here because of him — he talked me into helping him when he was tagging the school and I went along because I kind of liked him. He's hot, but he's a bad boy."

I fought the urge to wipe the smile from her face. I felt like a fool for having tried so hard to be nice to her. But I wouldn't let her know that, and I wouldn't be caught looking like an idiot. "Oh, yeah. Zach did tell me about that. I guess I forgot."

A knot twisted in my stomach and a sour taste formed in the back of my throat. I gave Rachael a soft smack on the back, laughing a bit too hard. "Partners in crime, that's what he said." I moved down the fence and found a new spot to paint.

I waited a while and then moved beside Zach. "You won't threaten to throw a punch if I get too close, will you?"

"Nah. I'm over it." Zach smiled. It was not as bright as usual.

"So, Rachael was just saying you two are neighbours. What's it like living next to a real live Barbie doll?" I pretended to flip my hair and wink a bunch of times.

"Her dad and my dad are good friends. That's it. We've hung out some, but she's not my type." Again, Zach attempted a smile. He began to gather up the paint and brushes. The painting part of our session was over for the day.

"How come you never mentioned it before? You said you didn't know how she got here."

"Look, there's lots we don't know about each other. Don't worry about it, Vic." His voice was angry and loud. Then his eyes filled with regret and he turned to me and took my hand in his. "Sorry, I guess I'm just worried about Dad and what might happen."

"It'll be okay," I said as we moved along the fence, picking up brushes and supplies. Despite the reassuring words, I was filled with doubt.

"Okay, we've got some more graffiti to remove," said Cathy.

Again, we piled in the cars and headed downtown. Russell and Peter went in the cruiser and Zach, Rachael, and I were with Cathy. I didn't really feel like talking to Zach in front of Rachael so I just took his hand and squeezed it. Zach squeezed back, like he agreed.

Rachael looked at us and turned away shaking her head. She was the first to jump out when we reached our destination.

"Hey, we're doing this guy a favour," said Russell, as he painted over a tag that was messy and hard to read.

"Yeah," agreed Peter. "You wouldn't catch us doing anything this lame." He laughed.

"Not anymore," added Rachael.

The next stop was different. It was a beautiful dragon done in neon greens and royal blues. The red eyes watched me as I filled my roller with bland grey paint. I felt my own eyes water as my strokes covered the image. *Such a waste.* I wondered who the artist was.

"This one's almost as good as yours." Zach stood beside me. "Sucks that we have to cover it up."

I nodded and turned away.

When we got back to the construction site, Zach's dad was already there, waiting, in his SUV.

"See you next week." Zach gave me a quick peck on the cheek and jumped in the passenger side.

I stood on the sidewalk and watched. I waved at his dad. His black hair was neatly slicked back, his eyes were the same turquoise colour as Zach's, but they were hard and stern. He had the same square jaw, too, but his looked to be so chiselled from constantly clenching his teeth.

Zach's father rolled down the window and spoke. "Listen here, Miss. I think it would be best if you didn't see my son anymore. He seems to have an affection for trouble and I'd say that includes *you*." His eyes raked me up and down, taking in my hair, makeup, and piercings. "He needs to clean up his act, and choosing a more suitable girlfriend is a good place to start."

My jaw dropped. I didn't even defend myself. It wasn't the first time someone had judged me based on the way I looked, but this was definitely the first time it felt like such a kick in the gut. I searched Zach's eyes, hoping he'd stand up for me, but he turned away. Where was the guy who stood up for me at Tim's the other night?

The window of the SUV rolled back up and the car took off smoothly, leaving me standing there, speechless.

TWENTY

"How's it going with the art project?" Mom looked up from her magazine devoted to news about the royal family. She was reading about Prince William, Kate, George, and baby Charlotte. Fascinating. I couldn't believe she had gone back to focusing on the royals when there was so much stuff happening here in the real world with me, Dad, and Elsie.

"Fine. We're close to finishing the fence. It's all about houses from the past."

Mom turned the page. "Will and Kate are planning another tour. Wouldn't it be exciting if they came to Nova Scotia?"

Thanks for listening, Mom. "Thrilling."

I opened the fridge, grabbed the milk, and took a big swig right from the jug. Mom didn't even notice. I thought I'd ignore her rudeness and pretend like she cared. "We all have different painting styles and it's awesome how they're all working together."

"Well, enjoy it while you can." Mom flipped the page. "It'll be the last of your painting."

I stood there and stared at the top of her head; she hadn't even bothered to look up. I remembered a time when she was interested in what I did. She used to watch James and I paint. She even tried it a few times herself — she had a keen sense of colour. Her paintings were more abstract; she used to say her art was about creating a feeling, not a picture. When she wasn't participating, she'd still ask us loads of questions. Why did we choose that colour? What inspired the idea? How did we know when the painting was done?

She always wanted to discuss what I was doing. How was school? Did I eat all my lunch? What book are you reading now? But all that was gone.

I waited. She didn't move. I couldn't get at her by walking away like I usually did — she'd just ignore me — so I grabbed the magazine, forcing her to look at me.

"I can't avoid everything that reminds you of James." My voice was loud and rough. I wanted to be hurtful. I wanted her to get it. "Besides, maybe a reminder of James isn't such a horrible thing. He wasn't all bad, Mom. And I know Dad is a painter too. So you might just as well accept the fact that I'm an artist. It's in my genes."

"Don't get mouthy with me, Victoria. I said you weren't painting anymore, and that's it." Mom took the magazine back. She glared at me.

"I wish you'd give up on this *perfect* family and pay attention to your real one. James left, but I'm still here. And Dad's right here in the city, too. I wouldn't even care if Will and Kate were coming for supper."

"I can't even talk to you." Mom got up from the table, clutching the magazine tightly.

I searched her eyes for answers, watching her anger fade and turn to pain. My frustration was gone, but my determination wasn't. "I'm going to keep painting."

Mom gave me one last look. For a second, she softened and her shoulders relaxed. I thought she might even apologize, but then she straightened up and left the room.

I sat at the kitchen table with my head in my hands, crying. The sun went down as I sat there, the room growing darker and darker.

Twenty-One

I filled my sketchbook with drawings during the week and started another one. This one was the beginning of my portfolio. I chose drawings that displayed my skills. Some highlighted my ability to use contrast, some showed tiny intricate details with fine lines, and some were more imaginative, "out of the box" cartoons. I even drew on the covers of my scribblers and the back of envelopes that came in the mail. It seemed being upset made me more creative. And the more I drew the more ideas I had. Art was the one thing I could count on. It gave me a place to go, a place to dream, and be anything, or anyone, I wanted. It also helped pass the time and gave me something to focus on other than my fight with Mom and the mean words from Zach's dad.

I texted Zach: "What's up?"

What I really wanted to know was why he didn't stand up for me in front of his dad the other day. There was no reply to my simple question, so there was no sense asking the tough one. It didn't seem right that he didn't even try to contact me. Surely he could find another phone to use for a single call.

I checked my phone every three seconds. I finally threw it across the room, only to run after it, just in case he replied.

I banged my tray on the cafeteria table.

Justine jumped. "Whoa. What's up?"

"Sometimes life sucks. It's like riding a roller coaster."

"Fill me in," she said, turning off her music.

I eyed Justine and noticed her hair was now lime green. I thought of all the things that had taken place and wasn't really sure where to begin.

"Let's see. I went back to see my dad again and guess what?" Justine raised her eyebrows. "He's a painter! Zach got arrested for stealing his father's car, he might have to go to juvie, and now he's acting all strange and pissed off. Oh, and I saw Rachael at Walmart with her mom, and the ditzy act is all a show she puts on to please her mother who thinks she has to look like a dumb model in order to find a 'good husband,' " I finished, putting air quotes around the last two words.

"Wow. All I did was write a science paper and go to work."

"Yeah. *And* I forgot to mention that Zach lied about Rachael. They're neighbours and they were together when they got caught. Want to switch lives? I would happily write your essays. Plus, I'm sure Mr. Habib would appreciate me being more focused at work again."

"Naw. Don't think I could handle it."

"No one asks if you can handle it," I said sagely. I ate my sandwich and continued to hash out the month from hell with Justine. It really helped. "Hey. Thanks for listening," I said as we finished up.

"Sure. I don't know if you noticed, but I don't really have a lot of friends fighting for my time. You're going through a tough time, but it's kind of nice to have someone to talk to."

"It is."

"And...." Justine reached into her backpack. "I got a *C* thanks to your help!" She beamed as she held up her math test.

"Awesome! Good for you."

"Yeah. Maybe someday we can hang out together outside of school." Justine looked at me shyly.

"Yeah, maybe." We just sat there quiet for a few minutes, and that was okay too.

When the bell rang we got up and went to class.

"Here they come again, folks," said Jeremy with his hand to his mouth, clenching a pretend microphone. "And what a disappointment: this season's latest fashion experts are still wearing black, black, and more black. But wait, the flashy pink mohawk is now a glorious green!" His eyes got big and he pretended to be impressed. "Way to change it up, girls."

I shot him a look and entered the classroom without replying.

I slumped in my seat, checked my phone for the millionth time, and shoved it back in my pocket. Looked like I'd have to find a way to make it until Saturday without hearing from Zach.

"What's up, Vic?" asked Kate. "You seem a little blue." I couldn't believe she cared, but when I looked over her eyes were filled with sarcasm.

"Blue? Are you colour-blind?" asked Mark. "There is no blue there. It's all black."

"Maybe black is the new blue," Jeremy added, and he laughed again.

I had enough. I didn't want to be their entertainment today. I spoke slowly and softly, turning to look each one of them directly in the face. "You know, sometimes your jokes are just mean. If you could take a moment to think of someone other than yourselves, you might be surprised."

No one said a word.

I got up and moved to an empty desk at the front of the room. As I sat down I heard the three whisper.

"Jeeze, Mark, maybe you should lighten up," said Jeremy.

"Who knew the black beast had feelings?" asked Mark.

"Just shut up, both of you," said Kate.

Maybe just saying what I meant was more effective than all the sarcasm.

TWENTY-TWO

The closer it got to Saturday the more excited I became. I woke up at 5:30 A.M., showered, dressed, put on my makeup, and grabbed some toast. I checked the clock in the kitchen — it was still only 6. I returned to my room, shoved some laundry in the hamper, and pulled the comforter up on my bed. I checked my phone: 6:15. *Come on.*

I was at the mural before anyone else and took a few minutes to really admire our work.

Peter and Russell arrived next.

"Hey. What's up, Vic?" Peter greeted me with a grin that lit up his freckled face.

"Just checkin' out our handiwork." I reached out and gave Peter a high-five.

"Looks good, doesn't it?" Russell said, brushing curls out of his eyes to better appraise the fence. "We aren't half bad for a bunch of troublemakers."

"Yeah. Your style's got flare, Vic." Peter pointed to the panel where I had painted a futuristic skyscraper.

My cartooning made the building of rounded glass domes look like it was centuries ahead of its time. Rachael had added trees as tall as the building, bearing fruit that could be picked from each balcony. Russell's lettering said "Halifax, 2050." This was one of my favourite panels; the rest of the mural was true to history, but on this one we got to use our imagination and dream of what our little city might look like in years to come.

"Thanks," I said, flattered. "Maybe someday you'll decide to use more colours."

"Nah. I prefer black and white," he said with a smile. "You understand."

Rachael appeared. "Hello, boys. Hey, Vic. What are you guys talking about?"

"We were just saying how much we like the mural." Peter gestured toward the fence, and then gave it two thumbs up.

"Who would've thought we could do all this?" Russell stood up straighter and nodded.

"I almost hate to admit it, but I guess Cathy's 'small steps approach' really works," I said. Bit by bit, we had brought our vision to life. We had incorporated each of our styles, and I think we even came to appreciate each other.

"Well, don't be telling the whole world we learned something," said Rachael.

We all laughed and almost didn't notice the two men in suits and hard hats approach.

One man spoke to the other and pointed in my direction. I figured they were comparing negative opinions of my look, and it pissed me off. My good mood vanished.

"Excuse me, Miss," he said, addressing me. "Are you one of the artists here?" he asked.

"What's it to you?" I shot back and moved down the sidewalk.

"Wait! We have a proposition for you," said the second man.

"What makes you think I'd be interested in anything from you?" I rolled my eyes. The others had moved closer to hear what the two men had to say.

"Sorry, Miss." The businessman stepped back slightly.

"I don't think you understand," said the second man, holding up both hands in surrender. "We wanted to offer you, all of you, the chance to paint another mural on our next construction project."

"Sure, man," Russell said immediately, full of enthusiasm. He nodded at Peter.

"Yeah, sounds good to me," agreed Peter.

"Completely lame. Count me out." Zach had appeared behind me.

"Yeah, no thanks," chirped Rachael. "It's not really my thing." She smiled at Zach.

I was so happy to see Zach, I didn't even answer. He looked at me and quickly lowered his eyes. He stuffed his thumbs in his pockets, suddenly transfixed with a stone on the sidewalk.

I was just about to reach for Zach's hand, but Rachael moved in. She put her arms around his neck and reached up to give him a peck on the cheek.

"Thanks for dinner the other night." Rachael giggled. "It was so nice to talk with you and your dad."

I froze. My throat got tight and I stared, trying to figure out what was going on. I looked at Zach, but he avoided eye contact. He watched Rachael as she sauntered over to the mural.

I walked over and got right in his face. "Really?" I demanded. "Suddenly, making Daddy happy is important to you?"

Zach shrugged and backed away.

I wanted to do something. I wanted to hit him. I wanted to hurt him like he had just hurt me. "Zach. Look at me." He didn't move or speak. I backed away. "Ken and Barbie — together at last," I called out for everyone to hear and raised my hands to clap. Why didn't he tell me before now? Why had he waited until we were here at the project and everyone was around? Even as Goth Girl, it was hard to feel mouthy. I felt stupid and humiliated.

"I'm sorry," he said quietly. "Dad invited her over. I was in so much trouble, Vic. I didn't know what else to do."

I swallowed hard, using every bit of strength I could find. I wouldn't lose my cool. Not now in front of everybody. "So that's it. You chose Barbie in order to keep your freedom. Good for you, Zach. I'm glad you're not going to juvie, but you can't just toss people aside to save yourself."

I wanted to run, get out of there, but I didn't. Instead, I willed my legs to carry me back to the mural. I studied one of the spots I had painted so hard I thought I might bore a hole in the fence. "So tell me, Peter, do you think I need more shading here?" I asked.

It took Peter a moment to catch on, but once he did, he went along with me. "Yeah. Maybe a bit here," he said, pointing. He seemed as surprised by Zach as I was.

"But not too much." Russell joined us at the fence, showing his support. "I think things are pretty much done here." He turned and shook his head at Zach. Then he leaned in closer and whispered in my ear. "Vic, the two construction dudes are still here, waiting for your answer." He motioned at the suits in hard hats.

I turned to the two men and put my hand out to shake on the deal. "Of course I'm in. Do you think Dumb and Dumber here could handle it without me? Not a chance." I looked back at Russell and Peter and winked.

Rachael and Zach walked down the street toward Zach's car.

I watched them for a moment and felt empty, like a gutted fish.

Peter, Russell, and I stood there waiting for Cathy. When she arrived we quickly got to work painting and avoided talking about what had just happened. No one answered when she asked where Rachael and Zach were. Every time I heard a car approach, I turned to see if it was them. I bet they were somewhere having breakfast and laughing at the dumb look on my face. I hoped they both choked on their eggs.

It seemed to take forever before Cathy let us go for the day. I was almost home when I heard a car pull over beside me.

"Vic."

I turned automatically when I heard my name. Once I realized it was Zach I turned back around and began to walk faster. I *really* didn't want to talk to him — the wound was still fresh, and I couldn't count on keeping it together.

He killed the engine and I heard the door open and close. Zach jogged to catch up to me.

"*Vic.* I'm sorry. I didn't mean to hurt you." He reached for my shoulder but I dodged and kept walking. He followed.

Then I took a deep breath and stopped. *I guess I might as well deal with this now.* I turned to face him. "Don't worry about it." I gave no indication that I accepted his apology. "I was just another way to piss off your dad. I get it."

"No." He tried to reach for me again, but I swatted his hand away. "I really like you."

"You have a funny way of showing it."

He stepped closer and took my hand before I could stop him. "Listen. You're a great artist. We had fun," he said ogling me. "I was just scared. Dad was right there. He invited Rachael and her father over and one thing led to the next." He tried that sketching thing with his thumb on my hand.

He pleaded his case pretty convincingly, but my mind was made up. I wriggled my hand free.

"No, Zach. You were only thinking about yourself. I can't believe I ever thought you actually cared. You're as phony as Rachael." I started to turn away. "You two make a great pair. Maybe someday you'll grow up and realize you can't use people."

I fought to keep my voice steady. Then I turned on my heel and walked away. I heard Zach call my name, but I didn't turn back.

Twenty-Three

I began to cry, feeling stupid for falling in love so easily and being so quick to trust some guy I barely knew. I walked around our block a few times, trying to calm down.

When I got home, I went straight up to my room and took out Zach's sketch of me. On the next page I had drawn one of him, but he'd never see it. This one was a real portrait, not one of my quick doodles or cartoon graffiti images. I ran my fingers over his bright smile and found myself smiling back. I closed my eyes and could feel his warm arms around me, his lips on mine. I thought about our time together and tried to figure out how it had disintegrated so quickly. I didn't come up with an answer, but I did realize one thing — Zach cared for me, and the proof was in his work. The portrait showed heart and feeling; each stroke had been carefully placed and blended to perfection. The likeness was spot-on, and even without colour, the charcoal showed depth and perspective. An artist couldn't fake this…I knew because my drawing of him showed the same things. It reminded me of the picture my father was painting. I wondered if he had finished it.

I went to the kitchen to find something to eat. Mom looked up from her seat at the table.

"Hello, dear."

"Hey, Mom." We hadn't talked since our big blow-up, and I wasn't sure what to say.

"I took a call from a man who said he worked at the construction site where you're painting. He said he got your number from Cathy, and he wanted to give you the location of the next mural."

I held my breath. If Mom told him I wasn't interested, that would be the end of it. I wanted to paint more than anything, and I would somehow, but I wanted it to be okay with Mom. "What'd you say?"

Mom looked at me and her eyes began to glisten. She reached her hand toward mine and squeezed my fingers.

"I took the address down and said you were looking forward to it. I told him you learned to paint from a friend of mine, but the real talent was all yours."

I stood there, letting the words sink in.

"What changed your mind?"

"I saw all the drawings you were doing on the mail and on your scribblers. They're good, Vic. It made me curious. I went over to the mural and tried to figure out what parts were yours. It's incredible." Mom shrugged and gave me a half smile.

"I know you don't have great luck with painters."

She winced and nodded. "And...." She turned and picked up a large rectangular package that was leaning against the wall. The brown paper was half torn off revealing the painting underneath. "This came in the mail yesterday." She pulled the remainder of the paper off and I could see it was one of Dad's paintings. I was little and running in the meadow. He had used soft pastel watercolors that were perfect for the picture. The muted tones made it look peaceful and content, like there was nowhere else to be at that moment. The colours were light and happy, just like the little girl. "I remember this day. You were so excited. I think you were chasing a butterfly. Look at the smile on your face."

I looked and I couldn't help but grin.

"You smile like that when you paint and even when you talk about art. I don't want you to give up your painting. Another mural would be great."

"Thanks." I hugged her. "I'll need something to paint because the fence is done next Saturday, and the city doesn't seem to appreciate my graffiti."

We laughed. I squeezed her tight and felt a genuine warmth I hadn't felt for a long time. Suddenly, I wanted to share everything that had happened over the last month with her. I told her about meeting Zach and how wonderful it was to be important to another person. Then I told her about Rachael. I started to cry, which made her cry too. I knew Mom understood my pain.

"I know it's tough, Vic, but you'll survive this. You're a strong girl." Mom sighed and took a deep breath. "I could learn from you."

I couldn't remember the last time we had talked like this.

Mom wiped her face and looked at me with tenderness. "Let's go see Richard."

I couldn't believe my ears.

"What?" I looked at Mom. Her eyes were still a bit red and puffy, but she was serious. "Are you sure?"

"I think so. It's been so long since I've seen him. He was once the love of my life, you know. And I *am* sad that he's sick." She squared her shoulders and raised her chin. "Besides, he's your father and that's reason enough."

We got to Elsie's house and knocked on the door. My legs were shaking and my heart was beating fast.

Elsie opened the door and gasped, "Oh my gracious."

She took a minute to see if we had come in peace, or if we were there for a fight. I guess she found her answer because she opened the door wide and let us in.

"Richard will be so surprised. And so happy." Elsie gave each of us a hug and led us down the hall.

I entered the room first. "Hey, Dad."

He was sitting in a chair beside his bed with his back to the door. He was completely focused on the easel in front of him and didn't turn when I spoke. He was just adding his initials to the painting in front of him. "Just in time."

"Guess who I brought with me?"

Still focused on the picture he replied, "I hope it's not some guy. You're too young to date. And besides, there's not a man out there good enough for my daughter."

His tone was so dad-like it made me laugh.

"You're right. No guy's good enough for me." I paused. "So I brought Mom instead."

He whipped his head around and his eyes grew big. He tried to stand but his legs were too weak. He wobbled and sat again.

"Julia." It was almost a whisper.

"Hello, Richard."

Twenty-Four

I got up early on Saturday. I walked down the hall and glanced at the awkward portrait of Prince Charles and Lady Diana on the wall. They smiled like all was well, but I knew it was just a sham.

I ran my hand along the narrow table underneath the picture, remembering when James refinished it a couple of years ago. He had scraped and sanded away the old paint and varnish, exposing the beautiful natural wood underneath. Now that I was putting together a serious art portfolio, I missed him even more. He was a great teacher, and I was grateful that he taught me to paint, but I also knew that even if he hadn't, I would have somehow found art on my own. After all, it was in my genes.

I went to my room and took the picture of Dad that Elsie had given me and placed it on the table. Two teachers.

I stared at my reflection in the mirror in my room. Today was the last day of the community art project. I decided to leave Goth Girl home today and let Vic Markham show up. My hair fell around my chin and my eyes were bright and visible. Not half bad. I grabbed a pair of jeans, reached in the back of my closet for a bright pink T-shirt, and headed out.

When I got to the hoarding, I admired our mural one last time. I strolled along the entire length of the fence. We really had created our vision of houses through time, from the early Mi'kmaw wigwams, through scenes of Port Royal, an Acadian village, Citadel Hill, the Hydrostone houses, apartment and condominium buildings, huge fancy homes, right through to my futuristic condominium skyscraper. Scattered amongst these main images were our representations of naval ships, universities, mobile homes, trailers, tents, and even an abandoned building that had been turned into a makeshift shelter. The different styles all worked together, creating a sense of community without losing individuality. I nodded and stood a little taller. *Good job.* We'd all worked hard and it showed.

As I stood there, Cathy and Officer Mitchell arrived.

"Hey, Vic," said Cathy, as if nothing was dramatically different about my appearance. "It looks good, doesn't it? You guys should all be pleased."

"Yeah, we did a great job. Who would have thought a bunch of brats could come up with this?" I smiled.

"I did," said Officer Mitchell. "I was counting on each and every one of you. Otherwise, this old cop might start to look like he was losing his touch."

I looked up at him and noticed a difference in his face when he smiled — the wrinkles became laugh lines and the grey hair hinted at his experience. He didn't look old; more like a proud father.

"Thanks for pushing me to take part in this program," I told him shyly.

"And I thank *you* for your hard work." He stuck his hand out to shake mine. "You're a great artist."

I shook his hand, accepting the compliment even though it felt awkward and unfamiliar.

The other delinquents arrived.

"Wow, look at you," hooted Russell, giving me the thumbs up and a nod.

I blushed, feeling like I'd been caught undressed and off guard. "Stop gawking and pull up your pants. I'm tired of lookin' at your underwear," I shot back. But then I smiled.

"Nice," said Peter. "Hey, Rachael, look at this. I think Vic's here to win Zach back."

I cringed. That's not what I wanted. Was it? I missed his lips on mine and the way his cocky smile made me melt. I missed texting him and talking about nothing. I missed *him*.

Rachael stood there with Zach, her mouth hanging open.

"So, wait. You think that now that Zach's decided to date a pretty girl, you should try to be pretty? That's a little silly, don't you think?"

It did sound silly. Zach looked at the ground and avoided my eye. That's when I knew.

"Nope. Not interested."

And I meant it.

"Well good, because it's too late, anyway." Rachael linked her arm through Zach's and tossed her head so her shiny blonde hair rippled in the wind.

Zach shook Rachael's arm away and stepped forward. "Hey, Vic. You look great." He put his hand out to touch my shoulder. "We could give things another try, couldn't we?" Rachael looked mutinous.

I stood there and stared into his beautiful turquoise eyes, but they didn't pull me in like before. "You'd really drop Rachael — just like that — and get back with me just because I changed the way I look?"

Zach looked confused. "Of course. I love that you would do all this for me." He reached for my hand.

I stepped back, astounded. "Rachael's right. It's too late. And you haven't changed a bit." I shook my head.

Zach hesitated, then turned back to Rachael. But she had already stomped off and was talking with Russell and Peter, her back determinedly to Zach.

Without another word, I returned to the fence to add my final touches to the mural. When everyone was satisfied that the mural was fully done, Cathy gathered us together. We attached an engraved plaque with our names on it, and she took our picture.

Rachael sidled up to me after the photo. "Hey, Vic, listen... I'm...I'm sorry about everything. I guess we were both fooled by Zach."

"Don't bother," I snapped. "I was fooled by you, too. You knew I was seeing him and didn't care! That bimbo stuff might be an act, but you being self-centred is genuine."

Rachael raised her eyebrows and started to back away. "Well, whatever," she said. Then she added: "but you *do* look pretty."

"Maybe," I said, "but it's not me."

I realized being Goth Girl wasn't making me invisible; it was expressing who I was and who I wanted to be right now.

After everyone in the group had said their goodbyes, I headed back to Leeds Street alone.

Alone in my room, I stared at the graffiti poster. I honestly did like the look of street art, and I wasn't ready to give it up. And I wasn't ready to give up on Goth Girl, either.

I grabbed my backpack and headed out the door. But first, I put on my foundation, lipstick, eyeliner, and mascara. I spiked my hair and smiled at myself in the mirror. I decided to leave the pink T-shirt on. I felt the rush of adrenalin as I headed out the door. I couldn't believe I was going to do graffiti again. In broad daylight.

I stepped out the back door. The bright sun was high in the sky with a promise of warmth. Two blue jays chirped happily.

I shook my cannon and the familiar rattle made my heart race. I took my time, making sure I got the details just right. The idea was unique, and the colours were perfect. I was so engrossed I didn't hear the tires crunching the gravel.

"Turn around," growled a familiar voice.

Startled, I dropped my cannon and listened to it roll across the driveway.

I turned around slowly, my heart pounding in my ears.

Then I laughed.

Officer Mitchell stood there smiling. He bent and picked up the runaway can. "Nice work." He motioned to my painting and handed me back the cannon.

"It's a new family picture," I said, just as Mom came out the back door of our house.

I had painted Mom and myself as cartoon caricatures, on an oversized piece of stretched canvas. My large eyes were surrounded by heavy black eyeliner and mascara. My black spiked hair reached out and touched the edges of the piece. Mom was snuggled beside me with a crown on her head, decorated with a little red cross. She was holding a magazine —*Learn to Paint*— and we both had huge toothy smiles.

"I came to let you know you have officially completed your community service hours," said Officer Mitchell. He handed me a letter, verifying my time served.

"Well, you're just in time to help us hang our new picture." Mom smiled. "It's going right over the couch."

I beamed as I finished the tag on the corner of the canvas — oversized bubble letters that read "Goth Girl."

ACKNOWLEDGEMENTS

I am not a great writer. I am not even sure I am a good writer. But I write, and write, and write. I work hard, listen, and learn. And I have been blessed with wonderful teachers, fellow writers, and great advice.

The idea of writing a YA novel overwhelmed me. The longest piece of writing I had done was 1,200 words. But Vic showed up and was determined to tell her story. A sassy young girl, dressed in goth, creating illegal graffiti, showed up in my imagination and I didn't know what to do with her. In school, I was the "goodie-two-shoes," the pleaser, the one who did what she was asked, when she was asked; Vic Markham intimidated me.

I did the only thing I could think of…I signed up for a workshop at the Writers' Federation of Nova Scotia. It was a course in writing YA with James Leck. I loved the workshop and the way Jamie used movie clips and pictures to help guide us. I was able to visualize separate scenes and now needed a way to string them together.

I applied for a mentorship through the Canadian Society of Children's Authors, Illustrators, and Performers with the creator-in-residence, Jacqueline Guest. I was accepted and she spent five months helping me work through the first ten pages.

Jacqueline's love of Vic and her encouragement carried me forward, but 40,000 words was still daunting.

I bought a book on outlining so that I could break my story down into smaller, manageable pieces. I read and read all of the YA I could get my hands on. Members of my writing group, Clare, Judy, and Carol, read many versions and were very supportive.

Once again, I came to a point where I needed outside help. I sent my manuscript to Marianne Ward, freelance editor, for an evaluation. Her feedback was invaluable. I had managed to get enough of the story on paper so she could ask the right questions and help me flesh out the details. She too, was enthusiastic.

Finally, I gathered my courage and sent the manuscript to Nimbus Publishing. It made its way out of the slush pile and onto senior editor Whitney Moran's desk. Although she liked the story and the characters, it was not ready for publication. She gave me some guidance and offered a critique, with no guarantee that she would accept it. I jumped at the chance. With her advice — and later, Emily MacKinnon's wonderful editing skills —*Goth Girl* became a book.

I also want to thank my husband, Jim, and my two daughters, Jill and Sam. They have always encouraged me to write and have listened to countless stories over the years. My girls are the two most tolerant, open-minded people I know. I have learned many lessons from them, the least of which is acceptance. This was the driving force behind this book. I learned to love Vic Markham and Goth Girl. I hope you do, too.

ABOUT THE AUTHOR

MELANIE MOSHER grew up in Amherst, Nova Scotia, and won an essay contest in grade two, sparking her imagination and beginning a lifelong love of stories. *Fire Pie Trout* received honorable mention in the 2004 Atlantic Writing Competition and later became her first published picture book. Melanie now lives in Gaetz Brook, Nova Scotia, and continues to make up stories to share with her granddaughter, Emma.